THE *Sea* IN *Winter*

ALSO BY CHRISTINE DAY

I Can Make This Promise

THE Sea IN Winter

CHRISTINE DAY

Heartdrum
An Imprint of HarperCollinsPublishers

ISBN 978-0-06-287204-3 (trade bdg.)
ISBN 978-0-06-307822-2 (intl. edition)

Typography by Sarah Nichole Kaufman and Catherine San Juan
20 21 22 23 24   PC/LSCH   10 9 8 7 6 5 4 3 2 1
❖
First Edition

To anyone who needs a reminder
that pain is temporary

1

SANCTUARY

February 15

I'm late to homeroom. Not because my bus was running behind schedule, or because my knee was flaring up again, or because of any other reasonable explanation. I walk into homeroom six minutes after the bell, because I couldn't force myself to come straight here. I couldn't walk in this direction. Couldn't follow the same path I go down every day.

My classmates are journaling at their desks. Several heads snap up as the heavy door latches shut behind me, as I hurry to my seat in the middle of the room. Curious gazes cut back and forth between me and the clock. Ms. Porter looks up from her own journal entry to beam at me and say, "Welcome, Maisie."

I drop into the cramped desk. Slender metal bars attach from the tabletop to the chair to the shiny tiled floor. Rooting the desk to this particular place. I fumble with my book bag. Pencil tips whisper against paper all around me, a gentle contrast to the coarse rip of my book bag's zipper, the obnoxious clacking of its buckles.

Seven minutes after the bell, I finally slap my composition notebook down on my desk and read the prompt on the whiteboard. Ms. Porter changes it every day. She shares quotes from famous novels, random facts about nature, or sometimes even song lyrics. Today, she has shared this word and its definitions:

Sanctuary
A place of refuge or safety; a place of protection
    from danger or a difficult situation.
A nature reserve; a refuge for wildlife.
A holy or sacred place; a building or room for
    religious worship.
Synonyms: haven, harbor, retreat, shelter,
    immunity, asylum.

I stare at the words. Flip to the next open space in my notebook. Pause, with my pencil hovering above the blank page.

I never really know how to begin these entries. Ms. Porter always tells us to be creative and open and free, to write or draw or spill whatever we're feeling, as we feel it. She never reads what we write; there are no grades in homeroom, just attendance and participation points. It's also our only fifteen-minute period, which means that I have about eight minutes left to do this.

Sanctuary. I write the word across the top of the page. Underline it twice.

Hesitate.

And then, in a messier scrawl, I write: *My ballet school has always been my sanctuary.* I stare at this sentence. Tap my eraser against my chin. Suck in a deep breath and continue on: *In the studio, I don't have to worry about anything else that's happening in my life, or in the world around me.*

From there, the words flow through me. I describe the bright, airy space in my favorite studio. The mirror-lined wall, the tall ceiling, the wide windows. The aluminum barres, the grand piano in the corner, the squeaky pearl-gray floors. The openness of it. The peacefulness of it.

I describe what it's like to dance in a room like that. To move through the sweeping gestures of a grand port de bras, the aching lift of an arabesque. To spin and step and reach as the piano notes pinwheel all around you.

From the front of the room, Ms. Porter claps and says, "Okay, students. Can I have your attention up here, please?"

I stop writing. Lean back as much as this rigid chair will let me.

Ms. Porter smiles. "It's Friday," she says. "And next week is midwinter break, so I won't see you all for a while. I hope you stay warm, happy, and healthy during your time off. Take care and have fun."

The shrill bell rings, and the classroom breaks into a flurry. I look down at the words I've written, feeling the yearning pull of them, like a fishhook in my stomach.

Then I close the notebook. Shove it inside my book bag. Stand up to join the stampede toward the door.

"Maisie!" Ms. Porter waves me down. "Maisie, can I have a word with you?"

I swallow. Extract myself from the chaotic

rush out the door. Meet her gaze.

She offers me a small smile and asks, "Did your bus driver give you a late pass?"

I shake my head. In an instant, the other students are gone, swept away in the roaring tide of voices and slamming lockers and sneaker squeaks down the hallway outside. And it's just me and Ms. Porter, standing in the awkward, muffled quiet of her empty classroom.

"Is your knee okay?"

"It's fine," I say automatically.

"Okay. Good." She gives an apologetic wince and says, "I have to report your unexcused tardiness."

I nod. Fidget slightly under her gaze.

"Try to get here a little earlier, okay? If it happens again this semester, I'll be required to give you an after-school detention. It's school policy."

I nod again. "I know, ma'am."

"All right. Have a good midwinter break."

She moves toward her desk, and I turn to leave the classroom. But before I step through the doorway, she says:

"And, Maisie? If you ever want to talk—if something else is bothering you, or if you need extra help with anything—I'm here. The school counselors are here. We all just want to see you succeed. You know that, right?"

I tell her, "I know." Even though I don't plan on talking to her. Or to anyone at this school, really.

She grins, oblivious. "I'm so glad. I'm always rooting for you."

2

CARRY THE X

February 15

By the end of the day, I'm frazzled and exhausted.

I wedge my way through the sea of students, between the locker-lined buildings and concrete pillars. The walls around us are cluttered with construction paper posters, marker-drawn announcements for spring sports tryouts, and Black History Month events. Blinds are shuttered over the classroom windows. We shuffle past the small and quiet library, which is where I used to spend most of my free time, until that day in November when I heard rodents scurrying around in the ceiling above me.

I was still on my crutches then, but it didn't matter. I managed to sprint out of there.

The crowd pushes me out and away from the campus, and down the row of idling yellow buses. Their exhaust pipes rattle as they wait for us. The smell of bus fumes fills the clear air. My book bag is heavy, the diagonal strap digging awkwardly against my shoulder. I'm surrounded by bulging backpacks and loud voices and people who laugh as they shove one another. I keep my head down, keep inching my way forward. An eighth grader in a football jersey lurches against my side, and I mumble an apology a split second after he's gone. I tug at the fingers of my fuzzy pink mittens. I keep moving, careful not to make eye contact with anyone. Careful not to do much of anything.

I find bus 185. As I climb aboard, the thrum of the engine tickles the soles of my feet. The back of the bus is already packed with people. A boy in the last row is dribbling a soccer ball on his knees. He bounces it in a repetitive rhythm, a quick swooping arc as he pitches the ball into the air. I move past a girl seated with her head down, thick-padded headphones on, her music turned loud enough for me to hear the shrieking lyrics.

I reach my own empty seat and slide across the mud-colored vinyl. My book bag hits the floor with a thud. I unbuckle its pouch, reaching for my cell phone. As I pick through the mess of loose papers, snack bar wrappers, and composition notebooks, I glimpse my graded math test. The one I just received in my last class period.

I barely looked at it when Ms. Finch placed it on my desk. But now, in the privacy of my bus seat, I can't help but stare.

Red dashes are scribbled all over the top sheet. The number 70 is circled beside my name with a C–. Arrows point between numbers. Answers have been crossed out. Beside the third question, Ms. Finch wrote: *Carry the* x. Beside the fifth: *You forgot to balance the equation.*

Shame prickles along my skin like goose bumps. I stuff the stapled sheets deeper inside my book bag, wincing as the papers crumple.

I grab my phone. Let the book bag drop. Take a deep breath.

There are three unread messages. Two are from Eva. The other is from Mom. I remove the mitten on my right hand to swipe my thumb across the touch screen, unlocking texts.

Mom: Hi, sweetie! Don't forget you have a PT appt this afternoon. I've prepped some snacks for you and Connor, so check the fridge if you're hungry. Veggies and turkey sandwiches. Mrs. Baransky will be over soon to watch him until Jack comes home (he's running late today, we both are, so much to do before our big trip!). Hope you had a great day at school. See you soon! Be safe walking home! Love you!

Eva: Just got here for the Jillana School audition. Wish me luck!

Eva: Also, Taylor says hi. ☺

I respond to Eva first by typing, Good luck at the audition. You're going to be great. Give Taylor a hug from me.

And then I tell Mom, See you soon. Love you too.

The bus doors flap shut, and we start to rumble forward. We jostle over speed bumps. We sway through sharp turns. The inside of this bus is humid, and the windows are foggy, so I open mine about an inch, relishing the cold snap of fresh air. The sky is covered in gray cotton clouds. The pavement outside is stained with wet spots that look like inkblots. It's starting to rain again. Tiny droplets splatter across the windows. The water streaks are short and thin as paper cuts.

I turn my phone over. Light up the screen, to see if Eva has said anything else about the audition. She hasn't. She might be in the studio right now with a number pinned to her leotard, grinning through the barre warm-ups to impress the Jillana School representatives.

I should be there, too.

We bump over ridges and uneven slabs in the road. The engine roars as we accelerate around a bend.

3

PUDDLES

February 15

I rise and exit the bus.

I thank the bus driver on my way out, as I always do. When my feet hit the sidewalk, I feel a tingle in my right knee, but I ignore it and move faster. Raindrops pitter-patter along the sidewalk. Parked cars crowd the narrow street. A pink balloon is tied to someone's mailbox, bobbing and tugging through the air.

I pull the edges of my beanie more firmly onto my forehead. Everything is gleaming and shivering from the drizzle. Dewdrops cling to the ends of bare skinny branches. Little waterfalls trickle through the sewer grates down the street.

When I first began taking ballet classes, we used to dance with colorful scarves. We'd spin around the studio with them clutched in our fists. We'd float them above our heads in port de bras. And at the end of each class, our teacher would gather them up and pile them in the center of the floor. She told us to pretend they were puddles. We had to jump over them, to avoid getting our ballet slippers wet. Then the piano music would start to play, and she'd clap to the beat for us as we would each skip, skip, skip, and *leap* across the imaginary puddle.

I wish I could go back in time. I miss how dancing made me feel. So creative and expressive. So quick and light on my feet.

I always had fun at my ballet school. There were never any bad days.

Until that final day, of course.

I trudge across the street. Cross our short front yard. Our neighbors might call our place Mr. and Mrs. Leith's house, which would be both right and wrong. Mom and Jack are married, and Jack's last name is Leith. But Mom kept her maiden name—Beaumont—through her two marriages. Each person in my family has a different surname: Angie Beaumont, Jack Leith, Maisie Cannon, and Connor Beaumont-Leith.

Our grass is overgrown and wet. Political lawn signs are anchored throughout the yard. Some of them are for candidates in local elections. Others are for causes: *No human is illegal. Water is life. Protect Mother Earth.* All of them are boldfaced, bold-colored. Streaked with raindrops.

I slog past them with my head bowed, the grass squishing beneath my feet.

4

THE RICHEST SIX-YEAR-OLD ALIVE

February 15

The moment I open our front door, Connor jumps up and yells, "Maisie! Look! Guess what I'm doing."

He is standing on the couch cushions with his hands locked behind his back. He's home before me, because he's had early dismissals all week for parent-teacher conferences. It isn't even 4:00 p.m. yet, but he's already in his Captain America pajama bottoms, and his short black hair is sticking up in all directions. His grin is full of mischief.

When Mom and Jack met with his teacher for their conference, she proudly reported that Connor is a confident and popular boy, with excellent skills in spelling and math. He's at the top of his class. But then again, so was I, when all I had to do was add and subtract for numbers less than ten.

"What am I doing?"

"I have no idea, Con."

"You're supposed to guess."

I remove my wet shoes by the door. Take off my mittens and matching pink hat. "You're hiding something."

Connor rolls his eyes. "Well, that much is *obvious*." He flaps his elbows for emphasis.

"I don't know. A toy?"

"No!"

I sigh and try to move past him, toward the dining room and kitchen. But he vaults from the couch to block my path, disturbing the cushions and sending throw pillows to the floor.

"You have to guess again."

"I already did. I give up."

"Just try, Maisie. One more time."

"Candy."

His brown eyes gleam. "Okay. But what kind?"

"Something you got for Valentine's Day."

"But *what* did I get for—?"

"Skittles? Butterfingers? M&M's?"

"Almost. It's a type of chocolate."

"Hershey's Kisses? Milky Way? Snickers?"

He can't take the suspense anymore. He lunges for me and lifts his palms in one quick movement, cackling triumphantly as he crashes into me. His small hands are stuffed with chocolate coins wrapped in golden foil. I wonder how long he's been waiting for this big reveal, how melted and sticky they must be right now.

"I'm rich!" he cries. "Look at all this money. I'm the richest six-year-old alive."

I give him a courteous smile. "That's great, Con. Now let me go. Please."

He moves aside, then follows me into the kitchen. There's a vase filled with camellia branches on the dining room table. They were Jack's Valentine's Day gift to our mother. He gathered them from the tree in our backyard. He claimed they were better than red roses from the grocery store, because those greenhouse-born flowers couldn't survive in the winter. *This camellia tree blooms every November and every February,* he told me. *That's the type of flower your mother deserves.*

Connor hovers behind me as I browse the pantry.

"Imagine how rich I'll be after I find my treasure at the beach," he says. He unwraps a coin and pops it into his mouth. "I can't *wait*."

"Yep," I murmur.

We're going on a road trip around the Olympic Peninsula. During this trip, we will dig for razor clams (or treasure, according to Connor) on the Strait of Juan de Fuca. We will hike the Cape Alava Trail (with permission from my doctor and physical therapist). We will visit Cape Flattery. And we'll visit the Elwha River.

I reach for a granola bar. Connor rushes to my side. "I want one! Can I have one? Can I please, Maisie?"

I grab a second bar, toss it to him.

"Thank you!"

I walk over to the dining room table, and he follows me, happily ripping his wrapper apart. I open mine too and start to chew. It tastes like chocolate chips and gooey oats mixed with peanut butter.

"Do you want to play with me?" Connor asks. The words come out muffled, because he's speaking with his mouth full. Which is something he knows he's not supposed to do.

"Stop that," I tell him. "How many times do I have to remind you?"

He ducks his head. "Oops. Sorry."

"Don't say sorry. Just stop talking until you're done chewing."

"Okay."

"*Connor.*"

"What?" he asks, his mouth popping open wide enough for me to see the mushed-up granola.

"Gross. Cut it out. I'm *serious.*"

"Hey, Maisie," Mom says as she comes breezing into the room. She's dressed in a worn flannel shirt and dark blue jeans. She kneads her long, wet hair with a towel from the bathroom. Her smile is soft and warm. "How was your last day of school?"

"Mom, Connor keeps talking with his mouth full, even though I've told him *not* to multiple times."

Connor's entire face scrunches. "It's not fair!" he wails. "I only asked if Maisie would play with me."

The corners of her smile droop a little. "Okay, okay. Maisie, you're not the boss of your little brother. But, Connor, you need to be more mindful of your manners. We had this discussion at dinner last night too, remember?"

"But—"

"No buts."

"But can't Maisie at least play with me?"

"Maybe later," Mom says diplomatically. "Mrs. Baransky is on her way over. Maisie and I are about to go see Mr. Lawson."

His small shoulders slump forward. "Mrs. Baransky? But where's Daddy?"

"Daddy is on his way. He had to do some maintenance work on the boat, and it took longer than expected. But don't worry, he'll be here soon."

Connor perks up. Takes another huge bite of his granola bar. He keeps his lips sealed as he chews, his jaw working in an exaggerated motion.

Mom nods her approval. "That's better, Connor, thank you." She bends at the waist, twisting her hair inside the towel, before straightening back up again. She walks into the kitchen, lowers the dishwasher's stout door, and yanks the top tray open, its contents rattling.

"You didn't answer my question, Maisie," she says as she tucks the colorful coffee mugs back into the cupboards. "How was school? Are you hungry?

Did you grab a sandwich from the fridge?"

"It was fine. And I'm okay; I ate a granola bar."

"Just fine? And are you sure?"

I shrug. "Yeah."

I finish my granola bar, toss the wrapper into the garbage, and turn to go down the hall.

"We're leaving in five minutes," Mom calls out after me. "Be quick, okay?"

"Okay."

I step inside my bedroom and snap the door shut before Connor can follow.

5

THE SHAPE OF A TRIANGLE

February 15

I change into a pair of shorts and swap my red winter jacket for a freshly laundered sweatshirt. I sit on the edge of my bed, slump back against the mattress.

Stare up at the ceiling.

My room is small and sparsely decorated. I have theater-sized posters from the Pacific Northwest Ballet's productions of *Romeo and Juliet* and *The Sleeping Beauty*. I have a bookcase filled with all kinds of stories: mysteries, fantasy adventures, sci-fi. I have a homework desk with a gooseneck lamp; a collection of cute, pastel-colored pens from Japan; and a tiny potted cactus. Fairy lights are strung across the wall below my window, clipped with photos from important moments in my life: being the flower girl in Mom and Jack's wedding, meeting Connor for the first time in the hospital, hugging Hattie and Eva after our final performance in *The Nutcracker*. We were still in our Polichinelle costumes and stage makeup. The thick eyeliner made us look like raccoons; the bright circles of rouge on our cheeks made us look like dolls. The overall look was pretty creepy, but you can tell we were happy.

Above my bed, there is a shelf with two objects balanced on it. An autographed pointe shoe from Noelani Pantastico, my favorite principal dancer. And a baseball mitt, signed by someone who played for the Orioles in 1997.

I inherited the mitt from my dad. It was one of his most prized possessions.

My parents had a short and tragic romance. The type of story that everyone loves to see in ballets or books or movies but hates to hear about in real life.

They were both Native, but they grew up in

different coastal communities, on opposite sides of the continent. Mom is Makah; she grew up in Neah Bay, in the northwestern edge of Washington State. My father was Piscataway; he grew up in Baltimore, on the Chesapeake Bay. Mom spent her childhood playing outdoors, riding her red bicycle around the reservation, and eating fresh seafood. My father spent his childhood going on field trips to the historic sites of Maryland, playing video games with his friends, and eating fresh seafood.

They both went through big changes in their teen years.

When Mom was fourteen years old, the Makah Nation hunted a gray whale. It was their first whaling voyage in seventy years. They agreed to stop hunting them when whales were listed as an endangered species. They waited until the Pacific populations were stable before legally asking for permission to resume this ancient tradition.

They received permission. But it was a controversial situation.

News helicopters buzzed above the choppy waters as the men set out in their canoe. The hunt was broadcast live on television. Protestors pulled their boats into Neah Bay. And in the days and weeks that followed, hundreds of angry and threatening phone calls were made to the tribe. Picketers carried signs and created bumper stickers that said: *Save a whale, kill a Makah.*

As the threats of violence continued, Mom's parents started to fear for her safety. They told her not to go out on her bicycle anymore. They told her to stay indoors.

After a bomb threat was made at her school, they decided the safest solution was to move to another town. None of them wanted to go; Neah Bay was their home, Mom was starting to learn the Makah language, and the whale hunt had brought the tribal community together. But my grandparents feared that the threats would continue. That they might turn into something real.

And so, over the summer, the family moved to an apartment in Tacoma. The transition was hard at first, but Mom has always made friends easily. As she attended high school in the city, she started a small Native American Pride Club on campus, where she met some Puyallup and Muckleshoot and Nisqually kids.

Meanwhile, my father struggled through high school. Mom likes to say that he was one of the smartest people she's ever known, but that he wasn't "good at school." He dropped out during his senior year, earned his GED, and then enlisted in the US Army. At the age of twenty-one, he was sent to JBLM, a joint military base south of Tacoma.

That was how they met. Mom was a student at The Evergreen State College. He was a soldier, preparing for his deployment. Their paths crossed at an Indigenous arts market at the Evergreen Longhouse in Olympia.

Mom always tells me it was love at first sight. (I'm still not sure if I believe that part.)

They were married less than a year later. And less than a year after that, he was deployed to Afghanistan. We only have one picture of him during his tour there; it's framed on the mantel in our living room. In it, he's dressed in crisp white short sleeves, seated on the edge of his cot, misty-eyed and grinning as he holds up the ultrasound Mom sent him in the mail. It's so different from his official, buttoned-up, and serious-faced serviceman portrait, which we also have framed on the mantel.

Between those two photographs, we have the American flag from his funeral. The flag is folded into the shape of a triangle and displayed in a glass case.

6

DEEPLY UNDERWHELMING AND UNHAPPY

February 15

"Maisie!" Mom calls from down the hall. "Mrs. Baransky is here. Let's get going!"

As I emerge from my bedroom, I find that the front door is open and Mom is ushering Mrs. Baransky into the living room, apologizing for the nonexistent mess. Connor is yelling for Mrs. Baransky's attention, asking if she got any candy for Valentine's Day, asking if she likes chocolates. And Mrs. Baransky is laughing her easygoing laugh as she politely declines his offer of chocolate coins, then turns to our mother with a reassuring smile.

"The house is perfect, Angie. Honestly, it always is," she says. "And I got a box of truffles for Valentine's Day, Connor! Do you know what truffles are?" She meets my gaze across the room. Her round cheeks are pink from the chilled air outside. Her blue eyes brighten as she smiles at me. "Maisie. How are you, dear?"

"Hi. I'm fine, thanks."

Mom points at the throw pillows strewn across the floor. "Connor, was this you? Did you mess up the couch? You're old enough to clean after yourself, young man. Put them back."

"But I need to hug Mrs. Baransky!"

Connor launches himself across the room, hopping over the pillows on the floor, colliding with the soft curve of Mrs. Baransky's belly.

Mom groans. *"Connor."*

"It's okay, Angie," she says as she gingerly pats the top of Connor's head. "We've got this. And you two better get going! Don't want to be late."

"Right," Mom says. She grabs her purse from the hook by the door and peeks inside, shuffling through its contents. "Keys," she murmurs. "Keys, keys." She straightens and glances around the room. Pats the pockets of her jeans. "Where did I—?"

I spot them on top of the microwave. "They're over here, Mom. I've got them."

I walk through the kitchen and grab the keys, then circle back to the front door, where Connor has extracted himself from Mrs. Baransky to give Mom a goodbye hug and kiss. Mom hoists him up in her arms, snuggling him, pressing kisses all over his face.

"I love you so much," she says. "Be good for Mrs. Baransky. I'll see you when Maisie and I come back, okay?"

He nods. The moment she sets him down, he turns to me.

"Maisie, I need a hug from you, too!"

He comes barreling into me, his bony arms clasped around my torso. I hug him back, patting his shoulders.

"I'll see you soon, Con."

"And Connor," Mom calls. "You better put that treasure chest away, before the pirate comes home and finds it."

Connor gasps, horrified at the thought. He releases me and vanishes down the hallway with his shoebox filled with valentines. I follow Mom out the door. Mrs. Baransky beams at us, waving goodbye as she reassures Mom—once again— that the house isn't a mess, the pillows aren't a big deal, don't worry so much.

Outside, the clouds have darkened, but the rain has stopped. Everything is dreary and gray and gleaming.

We climb in. Mom flicks the key in the ignition, and the car sputters to life with a creaky sound. Cold air blasts through the heater vents, and we both instantly shiver. Mom twists the knobs on the dash, shutting the heat off while the engine warms up.

"So," she says quietly. "Do you want to talk about it?"

"Talk about what?" I mutter.

"Whatever happened at school today."

I shrug. "There's not much to tell. School is school. It's midwinter break now."

She hesitates. I can feel her watching me. I can see the concerned crease between her brows.

"What?" I snap.

"Nothing," she says. Then, apparently changing her mind: "How is your knee feeling?"

"Better each day," I tell her. It comes out sounding more sarcastic than I mean it to, so I take a deep breath and add: "I mean it. I feel so much better."

"Okay." She puts the car in reverse and repeats herself gently under her breath: "Okay."

This is what happened at school today:

I ate lunch by myself. As I always do.

In my US Government and History class, Mr. Sandman somehow knew I wasn't listening to his lecture. And so, he called on me. He asked me to tell him about the Treaty of Paris. *In what year was it signed?* I didn't know. *Which war did it end?* I had no idea. *Who was triumphant?* I said, "The British?" Mr. Sandman snickered and said, "That was a good, educated guess."

Ever since I tore my ACL in October and had the surgery to reattach the tendon, I haven't been able to do anything in PE. Dr. Hart wrote a note to my teacher, declaring me banned from "strenuous activities." And so I spent my time in PE seated on the bleachers, attempting to focus on homework from another class, despite all the basketball dribbles and squeaking sneakers across the polished gym floor.

In English, we're reading some boring old book, by some boring old dude, set in some boring old time period. It's filled with language that makes no sense to me. References I don't understand. Metaphors that make me roll my eyes. But I'm *required* to read it, because my teacher says it's a Classic.

School is boring; none of the classes mean anything to me. It's the strangest thing, to spend all this time in school—forced through all these mandatory lessons—despite the fact that most of these subjects lead nowhere. Why do I need to learn about the Treaty of Paris? How will this Classic Book I'm reading serve my life? When I grow up, will I ever need to do math? Will I ever use algebraic expressions? I seriously doubt it.

And does Mom *actually* want to know any of this? Does she really want to hear about her daughter's deeply underwhelming and unhappy existence in school? Does any of it matter?

I doubt that, too.

7

MR. LAWSON'S OFFICE

February 15

Mr. Lawson's outpatient physical therapy office is located in the same shopping plaza as a pizza place, a health food and supplements store, a tailor, a dentist, a hair salon, and an office for tax services. We park at the far end of the lot and hurry across the pavement, because we're late. We're always running late for these appointments.

The lettering across the glass door reads: *Olympic Sports & Rehabilitation Therapy, Bryce Lawson, LPT.* The bell above the door chimes as we walk in. There are leafy potted plants in all four corners of the room. Armchairs with teal cushions. A small table with piles of dog-eared fashion and lifestyle magazines. A coffee bar is set off to the side, below a rustic-looking sign that says: *Caffeine maintains my sunny personality.*

The receptionist, Marisol, and Mom are friends, because Mom makes friends everywhere she goes. They have long, loud, and sometimes serious conversations during my appointments. Last week, when I came back to the lobby, I found Mom telling Marisol about how many funerals she's been to.

I have no idea how or why they got into that.

Marisol greets us both, and she asks me how I'm doing, and I kind of smile and shrug and sit in one of the armchairs. Mom goes to the coffee bar, filling a paper cup with steaming, bitter-smelling brew. She and Marisol start to chat; I tune them out. I place one hand to the bare skin of my injured knee, massaging the muscles with my chilled fingertips. I wince and grit my teeth.

"Maisie," Marisol says. "I have a surprise for you, dear."

I look up. My hand drops away from my knee.

Marisol shuffles through one of her drawers.

Then she rises up, placing a stack of three books on her desk. She says, "Fabiana cleared some space from her bookshelves again. She said that you would love these."

A smile touches my lips. I stand and cross the room. The paperback spines are worn and creased; the titles are printed in matching fonts. I reach the desk and touch my fingertips to the top book: *Beyond the Wildflowers*, by J. A. Corsair.

"It's a trilogy," Marisol says. "Apparently, there's a show based off this series. My Fabiana couldn't put the books down, and now she's glued to the TV every week. I hope you'll enjoy them as much as my daughter did."

Gratitude wells up inside me. Ever since I became a patient here, Marisol has given me gifts like this. Books handed down from her sixteen-year-old daughter. I appreciate them both so much. When the injury was fresh and I was still struggling to walk or move at all, books kept me going. They helped me forget my own pain.

It's been a while since I read anything for fun. Mostly, I've just been stuck with that Classic Book for my English homework.

I meet Marisol's warm brown eyes. "Thank you."

"You are so very welcome."

I flip the book over and start to read the description on the back. *Thank you* doesn't feel big enough to show how I'm feeling right now. I'm so touched by this surprise gift. As I stare at the small print, I try to think of something more to say. Perhaps a message for her to pass along to Fabiana.

But before I can, the frosted glass door on the opposite end of the room opens. Mr. Lawson peeks out at us. "Maisie," he says. "Welcome back."

I take a seat on the exam room table. Mr. Lawson sits in his rolling chair across from me. He has a clipboard on his lap, a ballpoint pen in one hand. He clicks the pen several times as he focuses on my chart. Brisk little flicks with his thumb.

He goes through the usual questions. Each appointment begins with this brief check-in. He asks about how frequently I've felt the injury in my knee. He asks about the severity of the pain and discomfort over the past few days. He asks me to give each day a rating between one and ten.

I bite my lower lip. "And today, I'd give it a two."

He pauses, mid note-taking. "Really?"

I shrug. I mean, sure, I felt the injury a few different times today. But it was never painful or shocking. I was able to ignore it, mostly.

Mr. Lawson resumes his notes. "I believe it."

I look up. "You do?"

"Yes." Mr. Lawson wears rectangular black-framed glasses that magnify his gray eyes. He sets his pen aside and says, "I believe we're making steady progress. I've consulted with Dr. Hart, and we both agree. When you come back from your vacation, I think we can cut your visits down to half-hour sessions occurring once a week. How does that sound?"

I can't help but gasp. "Really? You think so?"

His voice remains soft, contemplative. "I do. I think you'll be fine with those hikes your mother asked about. And did you notice you're not limping today? Or at least you didn't just now, as you came down the hall to this room. Your gait was perfectly steady."

Perfectly steady.

Those two words fill me up with joy. I'm suddenly giddy and grinning, feeling electric, like a sunbreak bursting through a storm cloud.

I'm making progress. Mr. Lawson doesn't think I need to come here as often, or stay and work through my exercises as long. This is what I've been waiting for. This changes everything.

"Thank you," I tell him. "Thank you, this is— this is amazing news. This means *so much* to me."

"Of course. You're still in recovery, and we must be extra careful and attentive. I highly recommend you continue to do your exercises with the resistance band at home, just as you have been."

I nod, over and over. "Right. Totally. I always do my exercises."

"Wonderful." He gives me a kind smile. Then he stands, opening the exam room door. "Now, let's go build up your strength for these hikes. And before you know it, we'll have you back in ballet school."

8

SPINNING

February 15

Mr. Lawson leads me out to the exercise room. There is a wall-length mirror. The open floor is cushioned with soft black mats. Racks of weights, stability balls, and resistance bands are stocked along the edges of the room.

He instructs me through the usual exercises: repetitions to strengthen my quads, hips, and hamstrings; balance exercises to help with proper alignment; stretches to increase my range of motion. I work through them all with soaring confidence, newly aware of how far I've come since October.

I'll never forgive myself for the stupid decision

that led to my torn ACL.

I was at the studio with Eva and Taylor and Hattie, all of us dressed in the same white leotards and pink tights. We were early for our Intro to Pointe class, anxiously waiting for the session to begin. Studio B was open, the sleek metal barres pushed off to the far sides of the room, warm autumn sunlight streaming through the windows. Faint piano music filled the space from the accompanist playing for a different class down the hall. An upbeat allegro. We could hear the rhythmic thuds of the students practicing their petit jetés and changements.

Hattie had memorized a soloist part from *Cinderella*. She was showing it to us, humming the music under her breath as she moved through the port de bras and piqué turns. Hattie has always been at the top of our class. Some of the girls think it's unfair favoritism, since her mom is a former principal dancer, but I've never felt that way. I just think that Hattie is gifted and passionate. I think she works harder than most people do.

But then again, I'd be lying if I said I wasn't a little envious of her. Because in addition to being one of the best in our class, she also lives in a beautiful, artsy condo in downtown Seattle, a few blocks away from the big convention center, the shopping district, and the waterfront. And Hattie's mom had a barre installed along the wall-length window in their living room. So Hattie can practice pointe exercises and barre stretches at home, any time she wants to.

I love everything about Hattie's house. I love the electric-blue chairs around her dining table, which are all bent in unusual shapes. The wooden coffee table in her living room has a massive, cracked geode slice embedded in its center. Her sofas have scarlet leather cushions. A collage made of sheet music hangs from the wall. Dramatic black-and-white portraits of Hattie's mother in various ballet productions line the hallway, along with a procession of Hattie's school photos. She and her mother look so much alike, the dance portraits almost seem like glimpses of her own future. A psychic foretelling.

As Hattie spun in tight circles, Eva, Taylor, and I were all seated on the studio floor, lacing the ribbons of our pointe shoes around our ankles. Cinching them tight. Tucking the knots inside the satin folds.

In our regular Intermediate Technique II classes,

we did piqué turns all the time. But we hadn't started practicing them in Intro to Pointe. We were beginners. We only did pointe work once a week; in contrast, our technique classes occurred four days a week. And the majority of our Intro to Pointe classes took place facing the barre, going through slow and simple motions—pliés, tendus, gradual relevés.

But there was Hattie. Spinning on her toes like a real ballerina.

She dropped down from the last one in the sequence with a sigh. "It's something like that," she said. "Then Cinderella lifts up to an arabesque. She follows through, plants her foot down in front of her, and does a forward bend." She demonstrated this, stepping to an arabesque on pointe, wobbling only a little before she stuck the landing.

Eva sighed. Crossed her arms over her chest. I reached over, giving her knee a gentle pat. I knew Hattie didn't mean to show off, but sometimes her flawlessness felt like a personal attack. It was hard for the rest of us not to feel frustrated by her incredible footwork. Her effortless strength and flexibility.

Hattie glanced at us. She stepped out of the finishing pose and ducked her head, looking suddenly shy. "Do any of you want to try? It's not as hard as it looks."

Taylor huffed and said, "I think we're good."

"Same," Eva said. "I need to stretch."

They both turned to each other, picking up a new conversation, blocking Hattie out. They didn't even compliment her, or mention how impressive she was. Which didn't seem right to me.

Hattie turned to me with a hopeful smile. "Maisie?" she said. "Come on. You're stronger on pointe than I am. You're seriously going to be the next Noelani Pantastico. If I can do it, you totally can."

I looked up at Hattie. She often compared me to Noelani. She always said that I looked just like her. That I moved and performed like her, too. And I wanted that to be true. I wanted to seem like someone destined to perform as the Peacock in *The Nutcracker*. Or Juliet in *Romeo and Juliet*. I wanted it so badly.

And so, I stood up. And I went to Hattie.

9

TIME TO HEAL

February 15

We return to the exam room. Sweat has gathered on my brow from the exercises, and I wipe it away with the back of my sleeve. Mr. Lawson nods and jots a quick note to himself on his clipboard. "Good," he murmurs. "Very good. You're doing great today, Maisie."

I sigh with relief. Lean back against the exam table. Mr. Lawson pushes a cart beside me. There is a wide, flat machine balanced on top of it. The machine has various dials and buttons on it, and a small digital screen. We use it for the electrical stimulation therapy.

I stare up at the ceiling as he gets to work, powering the machine on and rolling it even closer. A question rises to the tip of my tongue. A question that has been on my mind, ever since the beginning of our appointment.

When I began physical therapy a few months ago, Mr. Lawson said that it would be unlikely for me to return to ballet lessons this school year. He seemed to think that I would have to wait until next year.

But considering our progress, has Mr. Lawson's opinion changed? Would it be possible for me to return to ballet in the spring? Or the summer?

Mr. Lawson presses four cold, sticky pads to the bare skin around my right knee. Each pad is connected to a wire, and to the machine.

Mr. Lawson must sense my thoughts hovering in the air between us, because he says, "You're rather quiet, all of a sudden."

I try not to wince as he presses the last pad just below my knee. "Actually, Mr. Lawson, there's something I'd like to ask you."

"Ask away."

"Since—since I'm making such good progress, with the recovery and everything . . . do you think . . . when you said, 'Before you know it, we'll have you back in ballet school,' what did that mean? Exactly?"

"Ah." He frowns slightly. "I didn't mean to get your hopes up, Maisie. I know how badly you want to get back to the studio. But I stand by my initial estimates. I don't think you should return to your ballet lessons until the next school year begins."

I nod and swallow my disappointment. "Okay," I say. "That makes sense."

He turns to the machine. Gives one of the dials a slow turn. I feel the prickling course of electric currents, the cool pads warming against my skin.

"Can I ask another question?"

"Of course."

"Do you think I might be okay to go back this summer? Before the next school year begins?" His brow wrinkles, and I charge ahead to explain myself: "I'm only asking because the audition season has started. All the best ballet schools in the country are recruiting students for their summer programs. They'll be holding tryouts through the end of spring."

My heart starts to race, just at the thought

of it. We've already convinced Dr. Hart and Mr. Lawson that I will be okay to go hiking next week. What if we can convince him to let me do an audition or two? That's all I would want. It's all I would need.

"Hmm." Mr. Lawson tilts his head. "I'm not going to give you a direct answer right now. But I don't think this goal would be too unreasonable, as long as your recovery continues on the way it has been."

At these words, my heart leaps.

"However, I want you to be gentle with yourself. Trauma takes time to heal."

I'm quick to say, "I know! Believe me, I know. I'm being careful." I close my eyes for a moment, focusing on the electric pulses. "Little higher."

He increases the voltage. My muscles twinge in response. The pads grow even warmer. I open my eyes, blinking up at the ceiling.

"Right there," I tell him. "Perfect."

He nods once. Steps back from the machine. "I'll see you in twenty minutes."

He leaves the room, and I let my eyelids flutter shut again. I relax against the exam table's stiff cushions. My mind wanders as the electrical pulses buzz and swirl along my skin, gently twitching the muscles around my knee.

I daydream about audition numbers pinned to my leotard. I imagine the soft gray glow of the studio. The twirling melody of a piano.

10

OBLIVIOUS I

February 15

Twenty minutes later, the machine beeps and shuts off. My right knee feels warm and tingly. I point and flex my foot, stretching and tensing through my entire leg as much as I can. It's a relief to feel my muscles work, to feel the firmness in my calves, the arch of my foot.

Mr. Lawson returns to remove the pads from my skin. He reminds me to practice my exercises at home and tells me to have fun on the road trip with my family.

When I return to the lobby, I find Mom leaning

against the front desk, nodding as Marisol speaks. Marisol's voice is hushed, her words rapid and anxious. Her curls bounce as she shakes her head.

"—and with everything else going on, I just don't want to see her bomb this test too, you know? Her entire future depends on it. That's what's at stake here. Her future."

"I know," Mom murmurs. "I get it."

Marisol sighs. "She's a smart girl. She's capable of so much. I just wish she understood how important it is to go to college. That she can strive to be something more than—more than . . ." Marisol glimpses me out of the corner of her eye and trails off, swallowing hard as she stares at my face.

I pause awkwardly in the middle of the room. Mom straightens to greet me, forcing a bright smile.

"Maisie! Mr. Lawson says that you're ready for once-a-week visits. Isn't that fantastic news?"

"Yeah." My response comes out dull-sounding, closed off.

"We're celebrating," Mom declares. "I ordered a pizza, and we'll have some ice cream for dessert. How does that sound?"

"Sounds good."

Marisol pulls up the calendar to book my next appointment. Mom retrieves a credit card from her wallet to pay for this one. She gives Marisol a reassuring pat on the hand before we leave, with a few urgently whispered words: "It's going to be okay. Everything will be fine."

Marisol nods, even though her eyes are still a little sad.

I pipe up with, "Thanks again for the books, Marisol. Tell Fabiana I'm really excited to read them."

"You are so welcome. Take care, sweetie. Be careful on this trip."

Mom and I leave; I hug the stack of books against my chest as I follow her down the sidewalk. "What were you guys talking about?" I ask.

Mom waves the question away. "Oh, nothing. She's worried about her daughter's SAT scores. She's working with a tutor, but Fabiana's still struggling."

"Oh." I think of the C– on my math test; my stomach muscles clench.

Mom leads the way into the pizza place. When we walk in, there are two slim cardboard boxes on the counter waiting for us. I pull my phone out of my pocket to check for messages from Eva.

Eva: OMG IT WAS AMAZING. I THINK I DID AMAZING. WOW.

Eva: That was my best audition yet. Hands down.

Eva: Omg I'm so excited. I hope I got in!

I type back, Congrats! I hope they accept you too. So proud of you.

Even though I mean every word, my heart turns to lead in my chest as I hit send. A lump rises in the base of my throat, tightening my airway and shortening my breaths to shallow gulps.

Mom is oblivious as she thanks the restaurant workers and scoops the pizza boxes into her arms. She doesn't even meet my gaze as she hurries us back outside and to the car, talking the whole way about how she needs to finish packing for our trip, and how she couldn't find Connor's hiking boots this morning, so she hopes that Jack will know where they are.

We climb in, I place my new books in the back seat, and she sets the warm boxes on my lap.

"Hold them level," she says. "Please."

I shakily inhale the scents of garlic and marinara sauce. Mom pulls out of her parking spot and starts drumming her thumbs against the steering wheel as she inches through the traffic to exit.

   We drive all the way home, and I don't say a single word. I just sit here, waiting for my breaths to even out. Waiting for this sudden pang in my chest to go away.

11

CAPE WOMAN AND THE RIVER MEN

February 15

My parents had a love story similar to Romeo and Juliet's: short, tragic, star-crossed.

But Mom and Jack? They're more like Cinderella and Prince Charming: proof that even after losses and heartbreak, happily-ever-after can be possible.

Jack grew up in the city of Port Angeles, about two hours east of Neah Bay. He is Native too, an enrolled citizen of the Lower Elwha Klallam Tribe. Jack is the type of person who knows a little bit about everything, but he knows everything about Klallam and Pacific Northwest history. Probably because he was raised by his grandfather. His see-yah.

"I was only allowed to call him See-yah," Jack told me once. "Never Grandpa. He thought the English words for grandparents sounded ugly. But you know, sometimes when I was trying to be funny, I'd call him Gramps. Just to see the look on his face." He chuckled at the memory. "God, I miss him and the looks he used to give me."

Jack's see-yah was born on the Ediz Hook—a sandbar that extends into the Strait of Juan de Fuca—in 1928. At that point, his family was homeless. Landless. Like many other Klallam people.

"The late 1800s and early 1900s were a difficult time for the people," Jack explained to me. "Settlers were coming in, and there were all kinds of epidemics. Our ancestors suffered from smallpox, measles, influenza. Construction began on the Elwha Dam. And laws were passed that made fishing illegal for Natives. They weren't supposed to hunt or fish in the rivers or off the beaches around their traditional villages. Not even to feed their families. The state required special licenses to fish, and you had to be an American citizen in order to apply for a license. But we weren't US citizens until 1924. Natives could be arrested if they were found fishing outside the system. Just like they could be arrested for refusing to send their kids to the boarding schools."

The early years of his see-yah's life were difficult. The family lived in poverty. They were forcibly removed from Ediz Hook by white settlers when Jack's see-yah was only a small child.

"His family didn't want to leave him, but they were hungry, and homeless, and of course, there was the threat of going to jail if they didn't give him up. And so, he went to the Chemawa Indian School in Salem, Oregon."

This was where Jack's see-yah learned to speak English. Where he was forced to speak it. His teachers tried to beat the Klallam language out of him.

"He never talked about it much," Jack told me. "Even as an adult, he seemed haunted by that place."

Jack can be the same way about his own childhood. About the years before his see-yah took over as his guardian.

"Hurt people hurt people," I've heard him say, especially in reference to his own parents.

Jack moved in with his see-yah when he was fifteen. Which was the same age he dropped out of high school.

"I'm not proud of what my life looked like back then. I was young and dumb, convinced I was invincible when I wasn't. See-yah helped to straighten me out. He taught me what it really means to be one of the Strong People."

In their language, the Klallam tribes are known as the Strong People. According to Mom, the Makahs are the Cape People. And the Piscataway are the People Where the Rivers Blend.

We have a running joke in my family, that my mother has a type. That she goes for the river men. Especially the high school dropouts.

12

THE PIRATE

February 15

The four of us are seated around the dining room table, nibbling at the ends of our pizza crusts and listening to Connor talk about his day at school. Every night, we talk about our days at work and school, and every night Connor has the most to say. Tonight, he's telling us all about this girl named Abby in his class, who slipped a handwritten valentine into his cubby.

He is obsessing over this card. The significance of it.

"And then, when we lined up for early dismissal,

I tried to stand next to her," Connor says. "I even told Joey, my *best friend*, to stand with someone else, because I wanted to talk to Abby. But she pretended not to see me waiting! And Sophie P. and Ellie started laughing." He stares at his plate, deep in concentration. "I don't get it."

Jack is seated in the chair beside me, directly across from Connor. He's in a short-sleeved black T-shirt, faded gray jeans. His dark hair is slightly ruffled, the grown-up version of his son's mischievous look. His hands are folded on the tabletop, his fingers absently twisting his wedding band. "Is it just me, or does this sound like an unfortunate case of unrequited love?"

Mom snorts. Covers her mouth a second too late to stop the nasally sound.

Connor blinks. Then he crosses his arms over his chest, annoyed. "What? No. It's not—*that*."

Jack grins. "Oh, good. So you think the girl likes you back?"

Connor's ears turn bright red. "I don't like her. I just wanted to know why she put the note in my cubby, instead of my mailbox."

"What's wrong with that?" Jack leans toward me and adds in a mock whisper: "Also, what's the difference between a cubby and a mailbox?"

"We made our boxes *specifically* for valentines," Connor says, in a tone that implies this should be *extremely* obvious. "We decorated them and set them out on our desks, and everyone went around the room to put stuff in them, including Abby. She even gave me candy! Here, I'll show you."

Connor leaps from the chair and dashes down the hall toward his room. Mom tells him to walk, not run, through the house, and he responds by hurrying across the floorboards on his tiptoes.

Jack wraps an arm around me, hugging me to his side. "How are you? You've been quiet tonight."

"I'm good. Tired."

Jack nods and rests his chin on the top of my head. I can feel his heartbeat against my shoulder, slow and steady and strong.

"I'm excited for this trip back home," he murmurs. "I think it'll be good for all of us."

"Agreed," Mom says. "I think we could all use a little heart medicine."

I can't help but frown. I wonder if Mom and Jack really do feel that way. If the Olympic Peninsula truly is heart medicine for them, considering what happened in their childhoods.

Connor comes tiptoe-running back into the room. His shoebox-turned-mailbox is cradled in his arms. Its surface is lined with hot-pink construction paper, covered in blue and purple heart stickers. His name is written across the top in glitter-glued letters. Beneath the drop slot, there are two more stickers—a soccer ball, and a soccer net—along with the word *GOAL!* in gel pen.

Jack nods his approval. "Great box, bud."

"Thanks," Connor says distractedly. He sets it on the tabletop and rips the lid off, revealing a mess of fun-sized chocolates and heart-shaped lollipops and red-and-pink wrappers. He grabs a small carton of Conversation Hearts and holds it up for our inspection. Like this is a crucial piece of evidence in some wild conspiracy theory.

"See?" he cries, pointing at the penciled inscription. "To me, from Abby. She gave these to everyone in class, but she only wrote a note for me, and she put it in my *cubby*. What does it mean?"

"Well, son. I think you've started something that can't be stopped."

"What? But I didn't *do* anything." He fidgets,

wide-eyed. "Unless—wait, do you think I should've written a letter for her? Was I not supposed to wait for her in line today? Was that wrong?"

Jack straightens, removing his arm from my shoulders as he gradually rises from his chair. "Oh, I'm not talking about Abby. I'm talking about the mistake you made just now. You've unleashed a series of events that must run their course." He lifts his right hand, his index finger curling into the shape of a hook. "*Arr.*"

All at once, Mom bursts out laughing, Connor shrieks, and Jack pretends to swipe for the box filled with candy.

"Ye've revealed yer treasure to a mad-hungry pirate!" Jack shouts in his pirate drawl. "Finders be keepers, ye bloody landlubber!"

Connor scoops the box against his chest, bending his torso in a protective stance. In his haste, he's forgotten the lid, and stray pieces go flying. I hear the *crack* of impact as candies skitter across the hardwood floor. Tiny folded cards flit to the floor like flightless butterflies.

"*Arr,*" Jack says. "Ye loot is mine."

Connor drops, scrambling to retrieve the fallen candies before Jack can reach him. Jack makes an

63

exaggerated show of trying to hobble around the table on his "peg leg."

Mom is laughing so hard, she starts to clutch at a stitch in her side. I laugh a little bit, too. But even as the laughter comes out, even as I'm sitting here with my family, with the people I love so much, I feel weird. Disconnected from myself. Like I'm not fully *here* with them, right now.

I don't know where that feeling is coming from. But it won't go away.

13

LITTLE CROSSING-OVER PLACE

February 16

We board the Seattle–Bainbridge Island ferry the next morning.

The alarm clocks went off in our house at 7:00 a.m., and after we all silently made a pact not to wake quite yet, the alarms beeped again at 7:05 a.m. Then Jack lurched down the hall, banging on our doors and shouting, "Get up, we're late. Need to go *now*." And the morning took off in a frenzy, with Mom and Jack brewing coffee and reading traffic updates and the overnight breaking news reports, Connor yawning theatrically, me double-checking my packed bags and my text messages, rain pummeling the roof and windows.

Today is rumbling and wet. On our way here, cars splashed through puddled dips in the road, trees bent to the whims of the wind. We drove through the crowded avenues downtown, where pedestrians walked with bowed postures, their umbrellas angled like shields against the gusts. Sleek carbon skyscrapers seemed to pierce the soft bellies of the clouds.

After we park our car on the ferry, we climb a narrow staircase. It's cold and loud on the way up, the sounds of the loading cars and the crashing sea spray echoing up the walkway. I clutch my red winter jacket tighter around my body.

Inside, the floors are lined with gleaming tiles. Vinyl booths border the boat's windowed perimeter. There is a cafeteria toward the back of the ship. Beneath the salty marine air, I can smell something like bacon grease and fried eggs, the smells of breakfast.

The four of us find a creaky booth and settle in to gaze out the window. The glass is sea splattered. The waves are storm colored, vast and gray and edged in whitecaps. The ferry rocks and sways in a gentle motion. I can hear the thrash and gasp of the Puget Sound, overlapping with the hum of the other passengers, the relentless power of the rain. Of the sea in winter.

Connor nestles against me. I have the window seat, and I can't tell if he's cuddling me because he's cold or because he's scared or because he wants to see everything outside. His bright yellow raincoat crinkles with his movements. His body is small and bony.

"Hey, Dad?" he says. "How does this boat compare to your pirate ship?"

Across from us, Jack smirks. He and Mom sit with their knees touching, their coffee tumblers still clutched in their palms. "My ship is quicker," he says. "This old vessel couldn't catch me if she tried."

The right side of Connor's face is pressed against my arm. I can feel his cheek lift as he smiles.

"When will you take me out on the boat with you?"

Jack hums, considering. "Someday when you are much, much taller."

"How tall?" Connor asks.

"Nearly full grown."

"Like Maisie?"

I snort and Connor twists to peer up at me, his eyes brown and sweet beneath a dark fringe of lashes.

"What?" he says. "It's true. You're twelve, and you're almost as big as Mom."

"That's because your mother is, um—vertically challenged." Jack softens his words with a gentle pat on Mom's knee. She scoffs and pretends to brush him off, even though she's smiling and obviously doesn't care about her height.

"Mommy's doing what kind of challenge?"

"It means she's short, son."

"Oh."

We all feel the moment when the ferry dislodges from the pier. Sometimes, if you take the ferry when the weather is nice and the water is smooth, it can be easy to miss. Sometimes, these departures feel effortless.

Not today. The giant boat jolts and drops, fighting the waves as we venture out into the open water. Winds slant sideways, crushing raindrops mixed with sea spray against the glass panes. The Seattle skyline looms behind us, all sharp vertical lines and blurry grayness. Down at Pier 57, the Great Wheel pinwheels and flashes through brilliant color patterns: electric violets, neon greens, siren reds. In the distance between buildings, I can see the bright yellow T shape of construction cranes.

Mom and Jack focus their attention on their phone screens. Jack is squinting and scrolling slowly, his brow furrowed in concentration; Mom is taking pictures of our surroundings. Connor loops his arm through the crook of my elbow. He snuggles more firmly against me. I take a deep breath and rest my cheek on the spiky-soft top of his head. Together, we silently watch the thrash and spattering mist of the sea.

The ferry ride is quick and choppy. And by the time we reach the dock on Bainbridge Island, Seattle has faded far into the distance. A rain-drenched mirage across the Puget Sound.

14

UNANSWERED TEXTS

February 16

We disembark and drive north.

We pass through small towns and quiet neighborhoods. We cross bridges standing on stilts over water inlets, red barns tucked deep within rolling meadows, a giant wood-carved bear standing at the edge of the highway. We follow winding roads through ancient green groves, woodlands filled with secrets and murmurs and mist. There are old, broad fir trunks with knobby twists in their bark. Slender, leaning trunks that are splotchy with lichen. Canopies of green needles. Dense thickets of wild briars.

The air tastes piney and sweet out here, so different from the city, which usually smells more like wet pavement and car exhaust.

The rain has slowed to a drizzle. The windshield wipers glide across the glass in an easy rhythm. Connor is watching downloaded episodes of his favorite TV show on a tablet in his lap with headphones on. Mom and Jack are listening to some politics-focused podcast. They both nod along with the commentary. At one point, Jack says, "This is the Twitter discussion I told you about." And meanwhile, I am texting Eva, before either: (a) I lose service, or (b) her Saturday-morning pointe class begins.

Eva: Did I tell you I'm trying out a new brand? This is going to be my first class on Gaynor Mindens. Really hope I like them lol.

Me: Really? Let me know what you think. Pretty sure I'm a Capezio girl.

I bite my lip as I hit send. My mind flashes back to that day I spent at the beginning of the school year, trying on pointe shoes in a dancewear shop in the U District. I remember the woman who explained the pros and cons and price differences of various brands, how she measured my foot and told me I have an exceptionally narrow heel. We spent at least an hour at the barre in her store, her cold fingers pressed against my heel, holding the satin tight to show me how each shoe would fit once the ribbons were sewn on. Meanwhile, Mom kept Connor entertained by showing him around the store, letting him sift through the multicolored leotards, the tulle-ruffled tutus, the floral headpieces and rhinestone tiaras. I remember quietly apologizing to the salesclerk as Connor clacked around in a pair of character shoes he found, then tugged at a belly dancing skirt that was displayed on a mannequin, its little golden coins clinking noisily with each pull.

Eva: I've already gone through like five pairs of pointe shoes this school year. They honestly wear out so fast. At least that's how it is for me.

Eva: Then again, Hattie has gone through eight? I think? So maybe I shouldn't complain, lol!

Me: Hattie also has extremely strong, arched feet. Her pointe shoes probably snap in half when she points and flexes.

Me: No offense to either of us, but our arches aren't nearly as impressive. Lol.

Eva: Very true!

I swallow hard, thinking of Hattie and her

perfect ballerina feet. Her golden-straw hair and blonde eyelashes and bright blue eyes. I click the backward arrow in my messaging app and scroll down to my conversation with her.

After I tore my ACL, Hattie felt so guilty. She felt responsible. When I was recovering from the surgery in the hospital, she visited me with a bouquet of flowers and a plastic container filled with freshly baked chocolate chip cookies. She hugged me and cried and asked for my forgiveness. And even though I said it was okay, I hadn't really forgiven her yet. The pain in my knee had been too hard to ignore in that moment.

It's been hard to ignore for months.

But now I'm sitting here, on the road to rainy, dreary Port Angeles. And I'm staring down at our most recent text messages, most of which have been from Hattie. And I'm thinking about how weird it is for us to go from the way we were to the way things are now:

(January 16) Hattie: Two weeks in, and I've already broken my New Year's resolution. Hope your January is going better than mine! Lol!

(January 18) Hattie: We did barre to music from Romeo and Juliet today. I recognized it right away, and it made me think of you. Remember when we went and saw it together? That was so much fun.

(January 18) Me: I remember. That was a great night.

(January 18) Hattie: Probably my favorite ballet, tbh.

(January 21) Hattie: Hi I'm bored. What are you up to right now?

(January 30) Hattie: Hey! What's up! Hope your knee is getting better.

(January 30) Me: Hey. I'm good. The knee is feeling fine. How are you?

(January 30) Hattie: That's great! I'm so glad. And I'm good, thanks ☺ I auditioned for SAB yesterday, and I was really nervous about it. Still nervous about it, actually.

(January 30) Me: I'm sure you're fine. If anyone could get in there, it's you.

(January 30) Hattie: Thanks, girl. That means a lot to me. More than you probably know.

(February 1) Hattie: Hi again! Hope you have a great day today.

(February 9) Hattie: Helloooo ☺

(February 14) Hattie: Happy Valentine's Day! Miss you so much.

I swallow the hard lump in my throat. I feel

like the biggest jerk in the world. Because I know I shouldn't have blamed her for what happened. I know I shouldn't give her the cold shoulder. It's not fair. And I don't like the feeling I get in my stomach when I think about it. The queasiness. The tightness.

But the truth is, I don't really know how to talk to her anymore. When I see her texts, I usually end up avoiding them, telling myself I'll respond later. Once the weird feelings pass. Once the right words come to me. And then too much time will pass, and I'll start to worry that I ruined our friendship.

My phone buzzes in my hand; a new notification drops down from Eva. She's moved on from the pointe shoes, and is now asking if I've watched *Catriona's Crown*, the new TV show she told me about. I reply that I haven't seen any of it yet, and she starts shouting at me in all caps, and I type back with lots of exclamation marks and emojis, even though the guilt and queasiness over Hattie continues to gnaw at me.

15
TSE-WHIT-ZEN

February 16

By the early afternoon, we arrive at our motel in Port Angeles.

The asphalt in the parking lot is dark and gleaming, its white paint strips faded almost to the point of nonexistence. Cracks spiderweb out from an indent near the sewer grate. We pull into a spot near the front office.

This building is calm and quiet and a little sad. The air outside is cold as glass.

Jack goes inside alone to get us checked in, and returns to the car with an abnormally serious look on his face. It makes the rest of us instantly anxious.

Mom lowers the passenger-side window. Leans across the center console to ask, "Is something wrong?"

Jack frowns. "Their elevator is out of order."

For a brief second, my first thought is: *And?* But then Mom and Jack both turn to me.

Connor lifts his headphones from his ears and asks, "Wait, what's going on?"

Jack says, "Your knee—"

"Is fine," I insist.

"Are you sure?"

Something inside me snaps. "Yes, *Jack.* Mr. Lawson has me do exercises that are much harder than going up and down stairs, I promise you. I've been doing squats. I've been using resistance bands. And we're about to go hiking on this trip! I can handle the stairs."

Jack blinks, surprised by my outburst. Honestly, I'm surprised by it, too. Embarrassed by the sharp tone of my voice. I don't meet Mom's gaze, but I can sense the lift of her brows. Even Connor stays quiet for a moment.

"Okaaaay," Jack says, drawing the two syllables out all awkwardly.

"It's not a big deal."

I push the car door open and scramble outside.

Unfortunately, there *is* a low pulse in my knee right now, a dull throbbing sensation that feels the way distant sirens sound. And because of this, I lose my footing, stumbling slightly.

Jack reaches for me reflexively, lifting his arm as a barrier behind me; I flinch away from his touch.

"I'm *fine*," I mutter. "My leg is asleep, that's all. It was a long car ride."

"Sure," Jack says, but his voice sounds hollow.

Mom and Connor exit the car in silence, and I avoid looking at everyone as we pull our bags out of the open trunk. I swallow my guilt and hoist my own over my shoulder, just to make a point that I can carry it myself. That my recovery is going well. That I'm getting strong again.

My parents need to see it. They need to start believing it. I haven't told them about Mr. Lawson's update yet. That in addition to fewer and shorter physical therapy visits, it's possible I could return to ballet as soon as the summer. That I might be okay to participate in at least one or two auditions this spring.

If Mom and Jack think I can't even handle a bag, or a set of stairs, there's no way they'll let me audition. There's no way they'll trust me on my own.

I ask Jack, "What's the room number?"

He says, "206."

I nod and lead the way. The motel is painted a deep shade of gray. Its rows of windows are outlined in bright white trim. Its doors are dark blue, with bronze number plates posted above the peepholes. There is a handrail leading up the concrete stairs, lined with thin white metal bars that have rusted in places, reddish-brown flecks peeking through the chipped paint.

At the top of the stairs, I'm embarrassingly winded, but I refuse to let it show. I keep my mouth sealed to prevent myself from gasping for air; I force my breathing into a steady rhythm. A light sheen of sweat forms along my hairline at the base of my neck as I move down the row of doors to find 206.

My knee is still pulsing, but it doesn't hurt. It doesn't feel terrible.

But as a person, I feel kind of terrible right now. That fierce surge I felt a few moments ago has already left me. Evaporated into nothing.

I sounded so childish. Childish and wrong.

Once I reach our room, I lower my eyes and step

aside to let Jack use his key. The door opens with a gentle creak, and we all shuffle our way inside.

The heat is already on in our room. Warm air blows through the vents, rattling slightly with the steady gusts. There are two queen-sized beds in here, pushed against the wall, with identical nightstands and lamps positioned on either side of them. Both beds are layered in stiff, thick blankets and way too many pillows. The comforters are the color of green olives, the fabric stitched with swirling lines. There is a long dresser against the opposite wall, topped with a plasma TV, an empty ice bucket, a small tray filled with travel brochures for Port Angeles, the Olympic National Park, and the Pacific Coast. There are two wide windows with sheer curtains, a closet with an ironing board tucked inside, a mini fridge, a mini wastebasket. A kitchenette with white cupboards, a white enamel sink, a stovetop, and a coffeepot.

Our home for the next few days.

Connor and I claim the bed closest to the windows; Mom and Jack take the bed closer to the door. We fall into a quiet rhythm of unpacking and settling in. Jack carries the cooler we brought, filled with cut veggies and sandwiches and juice boxes, and starts to transfer everything over to the fridge. Mom unzips her cosmetics bag in the bathroom, lining her preferred shampoos and conditioners along the edge of the bathtub, her skin creams and cleansing tonics across the counter. Connor sprawls on the bed—with his shoes and rain jacket still on, ugh—his tablet held a few inches away from his nose, glued to the next episode of his TV show, absorbing as much as he can until someone finally cuts off his screen time.

I sit in the armchair by the windows, refreshing my messages, but there's nothing new to see from Eva. There's nothing new from anybody. And as my family continues to focus on their own things, smoothly forgetting about the awkwardness over the elevator, I feel more and more like a lonely storm cloud. Like a dark and dreaded presence, hovering at the edge of their happy vacation.

16
END OF THE ROAD I

February 16

"There's a high-pressure system moving down from Alaska tonight," Jack tells us. "Which is good, because that means it should hopefully stay clear over the next few days. We might get lucky."

Mom gives an exaggerated shiver. "Clear but cold," she says. "What are the temperatures supposed to be?"

"High twenties overnight, mid-thirties to low forties during the day."

"Snow!" Connor cries. "Isn't that cold enough for snow?"

Jack shakes his head. "Sorry, bud. With the high-pressure system, chances of snow are pretty low. There won't be any clouds."

Connor deflates, his ecstatic grin shrinking at the corners. "Oh."

We're all seated around a table at a Chinese restaurant. The lighting in here is dim. The walls are painted a deep shade of red, a dramatic contrast to the sleek black chairs, the crisp white tablecloths. A golden dragon with long whiskers and a snakelike body is painted across one wall.

Connor's disappointment only lasts about two seconds, because our server returns to our table with a tray full of plates wafting delicious steam. My little brother actually bounces in his seat and claps as the food is distributed. The plates are piled high with golden-brown noodles, colorful cooked vegetables with tofu, and deep-fried, orange-glazed chicken. Each serving is accompanied by perfectly round scoops of white rice.

We all express thanks to our server, who offers a courteous nod before she departs. Jack unsheathes a set of wooden chopsticks, breaking them apart with a clean *snip*. Mom takes quick pictures of her plate and the table before picking up her fork.

Connor dumps soy sauce over his rice with a splash.

"Mmmm," Connor hums happily, crunching a piece of orange chicken. "I want to go to China someday. They have the *best* food."

"Real Chinese cuisines aren't typically like this, bud. We're eating Chinese-American food. It's a different thing."

"Really?" Connor squints at his dad, unconvinced. "How do you know?"

Jack shrugs. "I'm a pirate. Pirates tend to know these things."

"Have you been there? On your ship?"

"Haven't traveled that far yet myself," Jack says. "But I do business with Chinese pirates all the time. I'd love to visit China. I'm also dying to go see Japan. It's on my bucket list."

Connor stares at Jack, wide-eyed and fascinated.

Jack meets my gaze across the table. He gives me a subtle wink.

I smile back at him.

When I was Connor's age, Jack had me convinced he was an actual pirate, too. But a few years ago, I learned the truth. Jack is a geoduck diver. He drives his boat throughout the Salish

Sea, harvesting giant clams from the seafloor. He sells these clams to local restaurants (which is how he met Mom; she works as a server in a fancy seafood bar), as well as international markets.

According to Jack, geoducks are some of the hardest shellfish to hunt. But they are also worth the most money. Geoducks are among the longest-living creatures in the world. They anchor themselves into the sand, and can live up to 160 years or more. Jack says you can count the rings on their shells to determine their age, the same way you would count the growth rings in a tree's trunk. Geoducks are also among the world's rarest creatures. They only live here, in the Pacific Northwest. In the coastal waters between Washington State and British Columbia.

But there's a huge demand for these clams in Asia. Especially in China and Japan. That's where most of Jack's harvests are sent. That's why he claims to "do business with Chinese pirates all the time."

A short silence falls over our table, broken only by the clang of forks against porcelain, the obnoxious slurping sounds Connor makes as he eats his chow mein.

Then Mom brightens and says, "How's the food, Maisie?"

"Good."

"Oh, good. Very good."

Jack eyes me. "Since when do you eat tofu, by the way?"

I shrug. "I had it at Hattie's house. I liked it."

He shudders. "I've never cared for it. It's flavorless. What's the point of flavorless food?"

I ignore him and take another bite. But I can almost hear Mom thinking. Bracing herself to say more. I can sense it in the frenzied way she's scooting grains of rice around on her plate. The way her eyes keep darting to me.

"So. Maisie," she says eventually. "I received an email from your math teacher. Ms. Finch said that she graded those unit exams. She listed the class averages for each period."

My fork freezes on my plate. I stare blankly at my food.

On Curriculum Night at the beginning of the school year, my mom signed up for each of my teachers' newsletters. Sometimes, I really wish she hadn't done that.

"What was the average for my class?" I manage to croak.

"Seventy-six percent."

I think of the red-inked comments on my papers. The crossed-out answers.

Mom is waiting for me to respond. Jack and Connor are both staring at me. The weight of their gazes makes it hard to breathe as I finally admit, "I got a seventy."

Connor grins. "Whoa! Seventy? That's a *huge* number. That's so much, Maisie!"

Mom and Jack don't share his enthusiasm. They both watch me with sad, wary eyes.

"Maisie," Jack says, his tone heavy with disappointment. "You are so much smarter than that."

I drag my breath in through my nose, out through my mouth. For a second, I'm afraid I might cry. I'm terrified I might actually break down over something as stupid as a math test.

Mom's voice is tight as she says, "Jack—"

"I'm serious," he counters. "This is getting out of hand. First, we find out she's getting a D in history. Then the GPA in her last report card dipped to a 2.3. And now this? Wasn't this exam worth forty percent of her grade? Maisie, what's going on here?"

I shrug, unable to speak.

"Do we need to hire a tutor for you? Are you

having a hard time focusing in class? What about your friends? Can you find a study buddy?"

Friends? At this suggestion, I straight-up laugh. A cold, cruel cough of a laugh, because I don't have any friends in school. I only have the girls from ballet, who I never even see anymore, and who don't go to my school. Eva goes to a Catholic school; her curriculum has always been a little different than mine. Hattie also attends a private school, an "arts and humanities" school that rejects all forms of standardized tests. Hattie's teachers don't "believe" in grading rubrics.

"I don't see how this is funny," Jack says firmly. "Your mother and I know you're capable of more than this."

This is true. I'm capable of doing ballet. Which is so much harder and bigger and better than anything middle school has to offer.

Jack plants his elbows on the tabletop. Leans forward to meet my gaze. His brown eyes burn as he says, "I don't know what's happening with you lately. But I won't let you continue down this path. You are my daughter—"

"I'm not," I snap without thinking. "Not really. Not technically."

Mom gasps. Connor's fork clangs against his plate.

My skin instantly burns hot with shame. My throat tightens reflexively, as if my body wants to take it back. Grasp those words out of the air between us. What did I just *say*?

What is *wrong* with me?

"You," he says slowly, pointedly, pressing the word deep into my skin. "You are my daughter. When I married your mother, I made a promise. To her, to the spirit and memory of your father, and to you. To *you*, most of all. I swore that there would be no difference between you and Connor. I swore to guide you and protect you and teach you, to the best of my ability. To be stern with you, when need be. And this is one of those moments. I won't let you push me away. I won't let you talk back to me like this. And I certainly won't let you make the same mistakes I made when I was your age. This is it. The end of the road. No more."

I cross my arms over my chest. Refuse to meet his gaze. I'm embarrassed and miserable and I wish I didn't disappoint them so much. I wish I could erase my words from existence. I wish I could go back in time and redo the stupid math test. Redo this whole conversation. Redo everything.

Jack says: "Maisie, you will look at me when I'm talking to you."

I blink back the wetness. Barely peek at him out of the corners of my eyes. My breaths have turned shallow and tight. My heart feels like a clenched fist.

I'm sorry, Jack. But I can't speak these words without crying. So I just sit here, saying nothing.

"You need to start caring about school again," he says. "Get your grades up. Get your act together. Or we won't send you back to ballet, even after your knee is all healed. These are your options. The choice is yours."

17

X MARKS THE SPOT

February 17

The cold front rolls in overnight, just as the meteorologists predicted. When we leave our motel room early in the morning, the air outside smells like snow, even though there isn't a cloud in the sky. The Olympic Mountains and their rolling foothills loom behind Port Angeles. The sun hangs low in the distance, casting their snowcapped peaks in light shades of pink, and their wide, bare slopes in deep blue. The banks of fir trees below almost look black. And our surroundings are crusted in frost: the railing along the stairwell, the windshields of every car in the parking lot.

Connor and I sit in the back seat as the car idles. The frosted car windows glow teal in the muted light as he asks me, "Are you excited, Maisie? Aren't you so happy we're looking for treasure today? If I find any gold, I'll share it with you. I promise."

I tell him, "Yeah. That's nice. Thank you." But I don't have the heart to tell him there probably won't be any gold. Or any other treasure.

Mom is in the front seat, sipping her coffee and setting the GPS for our destination. Jack is outside, scraping the ice crystals off the windows in scratchy strips. *Kirshh-kirshh.* The frost gathers along the scraper's edge in a flaky white film; Jack clears it with a quick swipe of his gloved fingertips. He works his way around the car, his movements brisk and deliberate. I watch him without meeting his gaze.

I'm still not sure if Jack was being serious last night. If he'd really keep me from ballet until I raised my GPA. If he'd really do something like that to me.

It seems a little hypocritical, coming from a man who didn't finish high school. A man whose life turned out just fine, regardless of his education level.

But at the same time—I feel so guilty for reacting the way that I did. For saying he wasn't really my dad. Ever since those words left my mouth, I've been replaying them in my head. *Not really. Not technically.* The shame of it makes my skin feel tight. The wrongness of it makes me sick.

And I still need to apologize. I need to find some way to make it right.

But how?

Jack finishes clearing the windows and climbs into the passenger seat. He snaps the glove box open, places the scraper inside, and says, "Who's ready to go exercise some treaty rights?"

And even though I'm sure Connor doesn't understand what he means, he shouts, "Me!"

Jack grins. "Want to see something cool, bud?"

Connor nods, fast and insistent. As Mom pulls out of our parking spot, Jack does a quick internet search on his phone and holds the screen up for us to see in the back seat. He zooms in on the words.

"Maisie," he says. "Will you please read this aloud for your brother?"

I squint at the words. "I—I don't really know how to pronounce these names."

"Sound them out. You've got this."

I draw in a breath. "Yaht-le-min, or General Taylor, S'klallam subchief, his x mark." I meet Jack's eyes; he nods excitedly, urging me to continue. "Kla-koisht, or Captain, S'klallam subchief, his x mark. Sna-talc, or General Scott, S'klallam subchief, his x mark."

"What on earth are you looking at?" Mom asks as we roll up to a red light.

"An important document."

"What kind of document?"

"You'll see. Maisie, please go on."

"Tseh-a-take, or Tom Benton, S'klallam subchief, his x mark. Yah-kwi-e-nook, or General Gaines, S'klallam subchief, his x mark. Kai-at-lah, or General Lane Jr., S'klallam subchief, his x mark." I pause. Glance up at Jack's utterly unapologetic grin. "Captain Jack," I read aloud. "S'klallam subchief, his x mark."

Connor gasps. "Captain Jack? But Daddy's name is Jack!"

"That's right," Jack crows. "And your daddy is a pirate. So, what does this mean? What might the x stand for?"

My brother's eyes go impossibly wide. *"Treasure,"* he cries. "X marks the spot!"

Mom's voice turns suspicious as she murmurs, "Wait, those names . . ."

But Jack surges ahead and says, "Yep! X marks the spot, bud. This is a treasure map! Are you ready to see where the treasure is hidden?"

Connor starts to cheer. He claps his hands and bounces in his booster seat. The light turns green, and we jolt forward as Mom says, "Jack. Were those names from the treaty?"

But Jack is pumping one fist in the air and chanting, "Treasure hunt! Treasure hunt!" Connor chimes in, "Treasure hunt!"

"*Jack.*"

"Angie. Honey. I'm getting the kids excited about our history, and our rights—"

"You're pretending that the treaty *your ancestors* signed is actually a treasure map—"

"We're having fun! Look at him go. He can't wait to start digging at the beach."

Sure enough, Connor is still bouncing and shouting, "Treasure hunt!" He's completely oblivious to our parents' conversation.

Mom sighs. "You're unbelievable sometimes."

"And you love it," Jack teases, nudging her shoulder.

She nudges him back and emphasizes, "Sometimes."

We park at a trailhead and walk down the rocky beach. The pebbles crunch beneath our rubber boots. We maneuver over slick boulders and smooth white driftwood logs. Each step I take is slow and careful. Jack pauses at the flat edge of a giant stone; he extends his gloved hand to me. I slide my palm into his, leaning against him to keep the weight off my tingling knee as I inch my way down to a patch of sand below. He holds me up; his lifted arm doesn't even shake.

He asks, "You're okay?"

I nod in response. Then, as he starts to turn away, I softly add: "Thanks."

Eventually, we reach an open stretch of sand. The waves trickle and hiss across its smooth wet surface. The air smells of salt and seawater, braided with cold breezes. Connor does a full spin—his arms held out at his sides, the hood of his yellow raincoat drawn over his head—and says, "Is this it? Is this where X marks the spot?"

Jack chuckles. "This is it, bud."

Mom starts taking pictures. Anytime we go

anywhere, she runs out of storage space on her phone. She holds her phone high above her head, pointed at the Strait of Juan de Fuca, the pale blue sky. Then she turns, snapping pictures of the evergreen trees at our backs, the boulders we climbed across, the nearby tide pools.

Jack carried the clam-digging supplies all the way here. He drops his duffel bag onto the packed sand with a jostling *thud*.

"Are you both ready for a crash course in digging for treasure?"

Connor jumps up and down and says, "Yes!"

Jack grins, unzips the duffel bag, and retrieves a shovel. He hoists it over his shoulder and walks with confidence into the swelling tide.

18

DIG DEEP

February 17

The trick is to watch for bubbles and dimples in the sand as the shallow waves retreat. Jack is an expert at this. He explains that the dimples form when the razor clams attempt to burrow deeper underground. He tells us to be quick so they don't get away, demonstrating by plunging his shovel straight down in the ground, then heaving clumps of wet sand away. Water pools instantly in the newly formed hole. Jack isn't wearing his gloves anymore, and the thick sleeves of his jacket are rolled up to his elbows as he reaches into the muck. He pulls the razor clam out; its oblong body fits perfectly in the palm of his hand.

Connor gasps as the clam wriggles its short neck. Its flesh nearly matches the grayish-brown color of the sand. Its goldish-brown shell is curved and lined with textured rings.

"Simple as that," Jack says. He crouches beside our collection bucket; he murmurs a few words of thanks to the clam, for feeding his family. Then he sets it inside and picks up his shovel again.

"Do you always thank the clams?" I ask. A couple of years ago, Jack brought me onto his boat for Take Our Daughters to Work Day. I can't remember if he thanked the geoducks—the giant razor clams that he hunts for his work—or not; I just remember feeling amazed and a little grossed out by how big they were.

Jack removes his baseball cap with a flick of his wrist, using its bill to scratch the top of his head. "I try to," he says. "It's a good habit. It's important to express thanks to those that help us survive. And our clams have always done that. They've always fed and nurtured our people." He replaces his cap on his head. Looks out across the water. "I'm assuming you two know about how the Duwamish

Tribe saved the Denny Party's children by feeding them clam juice, right?"

Connor scrunches his nose. "The who did what?"

"The Duwamish Tribe? When the settlers landed at Alki Point?" Jack meets my gaze. "Ringing any bells?"

"I know who the Denny Party was," I tell him. "But I don't know what you're talking about with the clam juice."

Jack makes a face. "What the heck kind of history are they teaching you in school, then?"

Connor says, "Dinosaurs!" at the same time as I mutter, "The Treaty of Paris."

"Yikes. Well. Okay, then. I guess I'll be the one to tell you. When the Denny Party landed at Alki Point in 1851, they had a few babies and toddlers with them, including Rolland Denny, who was only a few weeks old. This was in the beginning of the winter season, and they were struggling. The cabin they were supposed to stay in was unfinished. David Denny was ill. One of their other men was missing. They were in a completely unfamiliar environment; they knew nothing about how to hunt or gather in this region. The women were so malnourished, the mothers were struggling to produce breastmilk for their little ones. And so, the

Duwamish went to them, and showed them how to feed their babies with clam juice. If it weren't for those clams, or the knowledge and generosity of the Duwamish, it's possible those kids might not have survived their first winter in the Pacific Northwest. Maybe none of them would have."

The waves rush back in, the water swishing and rising to my ankles. Even though my feet are safe from getting wet in my tall rubber boots, I can still sense the cold surge. It makes me shiver where I stand.

Connor's response is a small, clear "Oh."

Jack nods. Scans the shoreline for more bubbles. Taps the packed sand with the flat side of his shovel.

"Why the serious faces?" Mom shouts from her seat on a long, bent piece of driftwood. She isn't participating in the clam dig; she's content with taking pictures of us, and with staying far away from the freezing sea.

Jack calls back, "Just telling our kids about how the Denny Party survived their first winter out at Alki."

Mom sits up a little straighter. And I can tell she didn't catch everything he said over the sound of the waves, because she replies, "Oh! I love Alki!

So many great memories."

Jack smirks. Turns toward the sea. Chuckles under his breath.

"What's funny?" I ask him.

He shrugs, but he's still smiling. "Nothing. Our first date was in Alki."

Connor is absolutely shocked. "Wait, what? You and Mommy went on a *date* before?"

Jack grimaces. "God, bud. Of course Mommy and I go on dates."

"When?"

"You know—special occasions, the occasional Friday night. We have romantic dinners, and we go see movies. . . ."

"When was the last time?"

"It was just the other—well, it wasn't really . . ." Jack blinks wildly at the sea, his face scrunched in concentration. He visibly shudders. "Okay, it couldn't have been *that* long ago. Maisie, help me out here."

I ask, "How am I supposed to do that?"

"I mean, you must remember, right? When was the last time Mrs. Baransky came to babysit the two of you?"

"Like three years ago?"

"No. No way. No, no, no. What about that day I took your mother to the pinball museum? When was that?"

Connor says, "What's a pinball?" at the same time as I snort and say, "Really? You took her to the *pinball museum*? Is that your idea of romance now, Jack?"

"Hey, I know romance, okay? Remember the camellias I gathered for her on Valentine's Day? That was romantic. And thoughtful. And—"

"Free?" I give him a toothy grin. "Yeah, that was super nice of you. Women love free gifts on the most romantic holiday of the year."

"Okay, you know what? Valentine's Day is a Hallmark holiday. It's a cash grab for the greeting card companies, between Christmas and Easter—"

"Yikes, Jack."

"And I, personally, would argue that New Year's Eve is actually the most romantic holiday of the year. Because it's all about new beginnings and anticipation and fireworks. It's about setting intentions together, growing older together, sharing midnight kisses."

"This year, you were asleep on the couch before the ball dropped. In New York City. Which happened at nine o'clock in *our* time zone."

"I work for a living! I'm asleep by nine o'clock every night, and I—and I—" Jack whips his baseball cap off again. Gives it a brisk flap. Heaves a deep sigh. "God. Okay. That's it, I get it. I need to take your mother out on a proper date."

I give his arm a gentle pat. "That's the spirit."

He sighs again and stalks off, scanning the shoreline for bubbles. My smile lingers as I watch him go. And I'm grateful that the tension between us is gone for a moment.

I still owe him an apology, though.

Connor inches closer to me. "Maisie," he says softly. "Do you think—when Abby put her note in my cubby, was that a cash grab?"

My little brother looks up at me with wide brown eyes, and I can't help but laugh as I put my arm around his shoulders and pull him close.

"Don't worry, Con. It wasn't anything like that."

19

SLIPPERY SHELL

February 17

The wind picks up as we hike back to the car, a rustling hush through the pines and foliage. It whips my dark hair around my shoulders, the strands lashing against my cheekbones. Gusts of air and seawater pummel the rocky shore. Even with my base layers on and the stiff shell of my red winter jacket shielding my torso, I can't help but shiver.

Jack is carrying his duffel bag over one shoulder, the bucket filled with razor clams in his other hand. I caught one of them, and it was fun, at first. The rush of seeing those bubbles rise after the waves retreated. How I didn't hesitate to plunge my shovel into the sand, chasing the clam as it burrowed deep. How Jack and Connor cheered me on as I dug in with my bare hands, clenching my teeth against the cold as I gripped its slippery shell. As I pulled it out, revealing its body to the harsh winter sun, the brisk marine air.

But as I murmured my words of thanks to the clam and dropped it into the bucket, I felt a sudden streak of pain in my knee. I winced, staggered a little. Mom noticed right away, her head snapping up from her phone screen.

"Maisie? You okay?"

"Fine," I said, but the word came out tight, like the letters had been squeezed together.

Then I crossed the beach to sit beside her. And I explained that I was fine, just trying to be careful, just trying to be cautious with my knee, and also my fingers were cold, so that was enough clam digging for me.

Even so, she eyed me like a hawk. She watched me as I walked. As I sat beside her, she pulled a protein bar out of her bag for me and asked again if I was sure I was okay. I sighed and snatched the protein bar, popped open its wrapper in my fist, and snapped at her to stop worrying so much. Because I was fine, okay? I already told her I was fine.

And she said, "Okay." She turned back to her phone, scrolling through the notifications on the pictures she'd posted from our trip so far. Then she chuckled under her breath and held the screen up to show me.

It was a picture of Connor leaning on me during our ferry ride. Both of us were looking out the window at the stormy Puget Sound, completely unaware of the photo being taken. The look on Connor's face was dreamy, content. The look on my face was—closed off, unreadable.

Beneath the photo, there was a new comment from Alice Cannon, my dad's sister.

Alice Cannon: My niece looks so beautiful and striking in that red coat! And the facial expression is exactly like her dad. The resemblance. Omg. My heart almost can't take it. Please give her a big hug from Auntie Alice! Tell her I miss her and am thinking of her all the time.

Mom wrapped her arm around my shoulders, hugging me tight against her side on Alice's behalf. And I blinked in surprise, staring at the tiny profile picture beside these words, at the beaming, bronze-skinned, round-faced woman who missed me and was thinking of me.

It made my heart feel bruised. It made chewing the protein bar difficult.

And now, as we're climbing back across the boulders and driftwood logs, I feel the muscles around my knee burn and tighten. I'm trying not to concentrate on it. I'm trying not to worry about it. But it's there now, my knee throbbing as I balance across the bleached driftwood and step between the barnacle-edged rocks. Up ahead, I can hear Mom laughing at something Connor said. I can hear the clams sloshing and knocking around in Jack's bucket. I can hear the whistling wind.

The fine hairs along the back of my neck stand upright. Chills shoot up my spine. The pulse in my knee grows faster, more persistent.

I try not to think about what this might mean.

I try not to stumble or fall too far behind.

20

LESSONS

Back at the motel room, Mom cleans, then cooks the clams. They're simmering in a pan on the stove-top right now, swimming in butter and garlic and white wine. Linguine noodles are boiling in a large pot. Lemon wedges are piled in a small bowl on the counter. Mom is chopping parsley on a cutting board. The knife flashes with each deliberate slice.

Jack and Connor are snuggling on Mom and Jack's bed, watching a wilderness survival show on the TV. Some white dude is hiking through a rain forest somewhere in Central America. Connor looks absolutely fascinated as he collects and filters water from a ravine.

"Is there poop in that water?" Connor asks.

Jack says, "Those are sediments, bud. Just dirt and sand. All natural."

"But it looks like *poop*."

I roll my eyes and hold the tablet closer to my face, turn the volume up on the headphones. I'm watching the video tutorials Ms. Finch recommended for our last unit in class. Since I supposedly need to become a math genius in order to keep doing what I love. My dance lessons are the only education I really care about, the only lessons that will serve my future.

But I watch as the numbers move around on the screen. As the equation is solved for x.

It doesn't take long for my mind to wander. A neat line cuts through the next set of numbers, and I imagine the ballet barres set up in parallel rows down the center of a studio. The same steps are repeated, and I think of the mirrored, practiced movements of barre warm-ups: the diamond shapes of pliés, the long reaches of port de bras, the clean elegance of standing tall in fifth position.

I miss those classes so much. I miss feeling my muscles work through the movements. I miss the ebb and flow of the music. I miss breathing through the adagios and soaring through the grand allegros.

My phone buzzes in my lap, interrupting my thoughts; it's a text from Eva. She's raging about *Catriona's Crown* again, asking if I will ever catch up, because it's on right now and it's good. And it's important. And I need to see it.

I bite back a laugh. Lift my phone and take a picture of the TV. I send it to her with the message: Jack and Connor have dibs right now.

Her response is instantaneous: CHANGE THE CHANNEL

Me: They're watching something else!

Eva: Change it NOW! OMG!

Eva: Phillipe is about to confess his love to Catriona.

Eva: Omg he's saying he's never felt this way about anyone.

Eva: Maisie, you don't understand.

Eva: They can't be together, because she's royalty and he works in the stables.

Me: Sounds scandalous.

Eva: Listen. He helped her overcome her fear of horses. Catriona used to be terrified of them, because her brother was killed in a horseback riding accident.

Me: Yikes!

Eva: Omg they cut to a commercial break. I hate cable television. Why isn't this show available through a streaming service? Just let me binge it all right now, like a normal person.

I start to type my response, but Mom calls out, "Dinner's ready! Maisie, put your phone and tablet away, please."

Irritated, I delete what I was saying, and instead send a message to let Eva know that my mom wants my phone away. Then I click the screen to black and slide it back inside my pocket.

I follow Jack and Connor into the cramped kitchenette. The buttery garlic sauce smells amazing. Mom has already scooped servings of pasta and clams into four bowls, each garnished with sprinkles of parsley and squeezes of lemon.

Connor grabs his bowl with a cute, villainous little laugh. Mom is grating black pepper over her own bowl. Since the counter space is limited, Jack motions for me to go ahead of him. "After you."

"Thanks." I still can't quite meet his gaze.

The four of us find seats throughout the motel room. Mom changes the channel to the evening news. We eat our dinner and watch in silence, as weather and traffic updates scroll across the bottom of the screen, as the news anchors discuss the opiate epidemic, the severe winter storms happening across the East Coast, and the quirky first name that some supermodel gave to her newborn child, which has already gone viral on the internet. The news anchors chuckle and shake their heads as they read other famous people's rude comments about it.

Sometimes, the evening news feels like the worst kind of entertainment. Like we're all just here to witness each other's tragedies. Or to make fun of other people's choices. To make us all feel crushed and frustrated. To remind us that we live in an uncaring world.

It's too much.

As if she can read my mind, Mom changes the channel again, settling on a trivia game show.

I twist the noodles around the edge of my fork. Mom and Jack and Connor are playing along with the game, shouting and laughing and guessing the answers. There's a dribble of sauce smeared down Connor's chin, because he's getting too excited and keeps missing his mouth as he eats.

21

ICE MACHINE

February 17

My family is asleep, and my knee is aching. It's a surprising, bone-deep soreness that makes me wince. Makes me panic. Makes me toss and turn in the stiff bedsheets while Connor snores gently, his drool pooling on his white pillowcase.

The heater clicks on: a gust of warm air, rattling slightly. The sheer curtains drawn over the windows look creamy in the moonlight. Our neighbors in room 205 are awake, and they are watching an action film with car chase scenes. I know this because I can smell their microwave popcorn, and

I can hear the tire-screeching noises and instrumental sound effects and gunfire. All trumpets and percussion and bullets.

I check the time again: 11:13 p.m.

With slow, careful motions, I scoot to the edge of the bed. I glance back at Connor, but he doesn't stir as I slip free from the covers, the fabric whispering against my flannel pajamas. Mom and Jack don't flinch or open their eyes as I tiptoe across the room and swipe the room key from the desk. Open the empty ice bucket and remove its thin plastic bag. Then I ease my feet into my sheepskin-lined slippers. Pull a sweatshirt over my head. And I creep over to the door, slowly twist its knob, and quickly step outside.

The cold air blasts my senses. It's like being dunked in water, coming up gasping and spluttering. My breath forms ghostly puffs in the air. I cross my arms over my chest in a feeble attempt to keep myself warm. I move briskly down the walkway, advancing toward the alcove near the stairwell, my ghost breaths trailing behind me.

I pull the door open and duck inside. There are two vending machines snug against the wall, both of them illuminated in a fluorescent radiance, shiny with their rows of brightly colored snack wrappers and bottled sodas. The silver elevator doors are sealed shut across from them, each taped with "Out of Order" signs. And there is the ice machine, humming softly in the corner.

I open its drawer. Pick up the little scoop and start shoveling ice into the limp plastic bag. The ice cubes scrape and knock together. I give the bag a shake, knocking them around even more.

Then I leave the alcove, hobbling down the dimly lit walkway. The sky is a deep blue, and it's dark enough to see the stars. They look bigger here than they do in Seattle. And the mountains loom so much closer, their shadows broad and angular against the night sky. The snow on them glows white in the darkness.

My fingers feel numb as I unlock the door. I fumble slightly, inching my way back inside with less stealth than before. The door latches behind me with a *clunk*; my sheepskin slippers flop over as I step free of them.

Jack sits upright in the dark. I can barely make out his features as he blinks several times, willing his eyes to adjust. "Maisie?" he whispers. "Is everything okay?"

"Yes," I whisper. "Sorry. I didn't mean to wake you. I'm going back to bed."

He blinks again. Leans back on his elbows. "You're sure?"

"Yeah. Totally."

I cross the room to prove my point. If Jack notices the clinking bag of ice in my hand, he doesn't say anything about it. I set the ice down on the comforter. Yank the sweatshirt over my head and drop it on the floor. And then I burrow into the blankets, situating the ice against my throbbing knee, a tight breath hissing between my teeth.

A moment of quiet. We're both sitting upright in our beds. Blinking into the darkness. Not talking at all.

And then Jack whispers: "That popcorn smells so good."

I smile a little. "Tell me about it," I whisper. "I've been smelling it for, like, twenty minutes."

"That sounds like torture."

"Yep. Pretty much."

It's either a quiet moment in their movie, or our neighbors have finally turned the volume down. It's only a low murmur through the wall now.

Jack sits all the way up again, seeking my gaze

in the dark. "What do you think are the chances of your mom and Connor waking up anytime soon?"

"Slim to none." I side-eye him. "Why?"

"So. If—*theoretically*, okay—I were to go down to the lobby, grab a bag of popcorn, pop said bag in the cafeteria microwave, and *then* bring it back up here . . . would you and I be able to finish it? Without waking those two up?"

"Yes. Definitely."

Jack squints at me. Skeptical. "Are you sure? You *really* think we can kill an entire bag of popcorn, in secret, just the two of us?"

"One hundred percent."

"All right, then. I'll be right back."

He returns about five minutes later. My knee is cold and still throbbing. But it doesn't hurt nearly as much as it did before. Which is a good sign.

Jack walks in with a puffed-up bag of popcorn. It smells rich and golden with butter. He grins at me in the dark. Retrieves two coffee filters from the cupboard above the coffeepot. He eases the bag open, its paper corners crinkling, steam bursting through the ripped opening. He crosses the room and sits in the plush armchair on my side of the bed. He fills the coffee filters with warm, fluffy popcorn and extends one to me.

Jack grabs the remote and turns the TV on, keeping the volume below three bars. It's barely a whisper. I can't hear anything that's happening in this sitcom rerun over my own crunching. But I guess it doesn't matter.

"Cheers," he whispers, holding his coffee filter aloft. And I can tell from the look in his eyes that what he's really saying is: *I know that you're hurting. But you'll get through this. Don't worry.*

"Cheers," I answer, raising my own. And I hope he knows that what I actually mean is: *I'm sorry for talking back to you the other night. You've always been like a father to me.*

22
OBLIVIOUS II

February 18

In the morning, Connor blinks and rolls over and stretches his arms, his small knuckles grazing the headboard behind his mountain of pillows. He blinks again. Yawns. And as he looks around the motel room, his eyes watering from yawning so big, he says, "Are we having popcorn for breakfast?" His voice is raspy. Tired-sounding and confused.

Mom says, "Good morning, sleepyhead. And, uh, no. We're not. Popcorn isn't a breakfast food."

"Then why does it smell like popcorn in here?"

My gaze cuts to Jack. His eyes widen; his brows

pop up. There is an empty, deflated bag of microwave popcorn crumpled in the wastebasket. Our coffee filters and a few hard golden kernels left as evidence of our sneakiness.

There is also the damp bag that held my ice last night. Tucked back inside the bucket on the dresser, as if I'd never used it. I'd dumped the melted ice out shortly after Jack and I finished the popcorn. I shut myself inside the bathroom, emptied the bag into the sink, and then ran the hot water until there was nothing left.

Mom shrugs. "I don't know, Con. But if you get dressed fast, we can all head down to the breakfast buffet and have some more of those waffles."

Connor shoots upright. "Waffles! Waffles! Let's go get some waffles!"

I step into my sheepskin slippers, tug my pink beanie with the pom-pom onto my head, and follow my family downstairs to the cafeteria. It's a blank, beige kind of conference room, filled with banquet tables, coffee thermoses, fruit baskets, plastic towers of cereal, tiered plate stands, and stainless steel food warmers. I fill my paper plate with unappetizing pastries—miniature muffins, a Danish filled with some dark, unidentifiable jam—a banana with too much green along its curved rind, and a firm, cool-skinned orange.

I take a seat. Mom and Connor are in the corner, waiting as steam rises from the waffle iron. There is a man at one of the other round tables, broad-shouldered, dressed in a camo jacket and a trucker hat. He has a cup of coffee clutched in both hands, and is staring at the wall before him, apparently lost in thought. No one else is here for breakfast. This conference room feels too big, too empty.

Jack takes the seat across from me and frowns at my food selection. "Here," he says, rolling a few sausage links from his plate onto mine. "You need some protein."

The sausages are burnt and greasy. They smell peppery. They crowd my plate, butting up against the muffins, staining the starched paper with little brown flecks and clear spots of grease. I stare at them in disbelief. I'm kind of disgusted by how shiny they are.

Jack digs into his breakfast, oblivious to my discomfort. Oblivious to the fact that I didn't get any sausages because I don't *want* any sausages.

Mom and Connor come join us at our table,

where I am now nibbling along the edge of my Danish, while Jack shovels scrambled eggs into his mouth like his life depends on it. Connor scoots in beside me. His waffle is golden-brown perfection, its squares filled to the brim with syrup.

"So," Mom says as she sprinkles brown sugar over her bowl of oatmeal. "Connor's shoes were bothering him yesterday; I think his feet have already grown out of that size. I'm going to take him to the store. Hopefully we'll find some better shoes before we do the Cape Alava Trail tomorrow. Maisie, can you think of anything you might want? Any shopping you'd like to do? Or would you prefer to relax here at the motel with Jack?"

I catch the look in her eyes as she glances at me. The thinly disguised hopefulness in her voice when she suggests that I stay behind. Which means that she probably knows that I iced my knee last night. And she wants me to be rested before our hikes tomorrow.

"Sure," I mumble. "I can hang out here. I'll keep reviewing my math stuff."

She brightens and says, "Great! I think that's great, sweetie. You'll master that algebra in no time, I'm certain of it. My smart girl."

I look away from her. Take another bite of my Danish.

Mom finishes dressing her oatmeal, whisks her phone out of her pocket, and leans back in her seat to take a picture of our breakfast table. I sigh and block my face with my hand.

23

CHANGING WEATHER

February 18

Later, after we finish eating breakfast, after Mom
and Connor have left for the store, Eva sends me a
text that says: Omg have you heard?!

I type back, Have I heard what?

Eva: Hattie didn't text you?!!

Eva: She got in. She got her letter! She was
accepted into SAB for the summer!!

Eva: Hattie is GOING TO NYC!

I stare at my phone, watching in helpless awe
as Eva bombards me with GIFs and images of
New York City: the flashing billboards of Times

Square, the bustling streets and yellow taxicabs, the mint-green Statue of Liberty. Plus all kinds of celebratory emojis. An entire paragraph of exclamation points. A screen effect that rains confetti down over our thread of messages.

Hattie did it. She's going to attend the School of American Ballet. The school associated with the New York City Ballet. Her dream school. Her dream company.

Her dream life.

I'm sitting cross-legged on the motel bed, on top of the stiff white covers. My tablet is propped up on a pillow in front of me, the math tutorial videos continuing to play for no reason. Jack is stretched out on the other bed, his eyelids hooded, his breathing so slow and so deep, you'd almost think he's sleeping. But he's not. The TV is tuned to the local news, and he's watching as they go through stories about a fatal collision in Pierce County, a recent controversy involving some senator, and a nationwide recall on E. coli–contaminated lettuce.

This moment doesn't feel real. The weight of my phone in my hand. The confusing blur of sounds and sensations around me.

Hattie got in.

Frantic, I hit the back arrow at the top of the touch screen and scroll down to our thread of messages. I stare at the words *Happy Valentine's Day! Miss you so much.*

The queasy guilt makes my stomach churn.

Our friendship is over. She's received the best news of her life. And she didn't even bother to tell me.

And it's all my fault.

"Wow," Jack says. "The weather's changing fast."

I blink up at the TV screen. The meteorologist is on now, standing in front of a map of western Washington State. He motions with his arms as digitized clouds swirl in from the edges. Some of these clouds are colored green throughout the south end: Aberdeen, Hoquiam, Olympia. Then they turn to shades of pink and magenta, in the central Puget Sound: Bremerton, Seattle, Lynnwood. And the northern areas are all speckled in white: Bellingham, Mount Vernon, Oak Harbor, Sequim, Port Angeles.

"Looks like we might see some snow after all," he tells me. "They didn't expect this convergence. They thought we would have at least a few clear days."

"Wow," I murmur. Unsure of what else to say. How else to contribute.

"That's the thing about February," Jack says. "It's an unpredictable time of the year." He glances at me. "If there's too much snow, we can skip the hikes tomorrow." Which is really just code for: *Let me know if your knee is hurting.*

"I think hiking through the snow sounds fun." Which means: *My knee is fine.* Because it is fine. It needs to be fine.

I need to be ready for the auditions later this spring. I can't lose any more time.

Jack nods. Turns his attention back to the TV. "I hope the roads will be okay," he says. "I really don't want to miss out on this chance to visit the Elwha River. That place was so important to Seeyah." Jack pauses and swallows. "I wish he'd lived long enough to see them remove those dams. He would've been so happy. He believed that the health of the river reflected the health of the community. That's what he always told me."

The longing in Jack's voice pulls me out of my own thoughts.

I blink at him. "What do you mean? About the dams being removed?"

"In 1910, the white settlers started to construct the Elwha Dam. In the same year, they wrote new fishing laws that made it illegal for the Strong People to feed themselves. I've told you about that part before, right?"

I nod, remembering. "You said that only American citizens could fish in the rivers. And Natives weren't considered citizens yet."

"That's right. So the people couldn't fish, and the Elwha Dam was built, then the Glines Canyon Dam came soon after. These structures choked the river. Salmon couldn't migrate; they couldn't return to their spawning beds. And the landscape changed. The ecosystems changed. By the time See-yah was born, his family believed the river would never be the same.

"But in 2011, an entire century after the construction began, and about five years—" Jack stops. Breathes. "About five years after See-yah passed, they began the deconstruction process. It was the largest dam removal in world history. No one else had attempted anything like this. But in 2014, both the Elwha and Glines Canyon Dams were gone. And the river roared back to life."

"2014," I say. "That's the year Connor was born."

"Indeed, it was. All the more reason why I wish See-yah could have been there."

We fall into a thoughtful silence.

My phone pulses in my lap. Another notification has dropped down from Eva: Maisie? Hello? You still there?

I click the screen to black.

24

WHAT AM I DOING?

February 18

It starts to snow that night. But I'm the only one awake long enough to see it.

Earlier, after Connor and Mom came back from the store, he pushed the sheer curtains open. White-gray clouds had swept across the sky, blocking out the winter-bright sun and the pale blue horizon.

"Can you believe it's going to snow, Maisie?" he asked me. "Maisie, if it snows, can we have a snowball fight? Can we go sledding and make snow angels?"

"It probably won't be that deep, bud," Jack said. "But we'll see."

And now, the rest of my family is asleep. The motel is still and silent. There are no noisy neighbors tonight. No TVs on, no footsteps down the corridor outside, no car doors slamming in the parking lot. The only sounds are the heater clicking on, sighing warm air into the room. And the nasally breaths and occasional flinches as Connor stirs in his dreams.

Fat white snowflakes drift past the window, barely visible in the dark. The whorls are illuminated in the orangish glow of the streetlamps below. It doesn't look like any of them are sticking to the ground yet. The pavement is wet and gleaming. Puddles have formed along the edge of the road, little mirrored wells in the asphalt.

My phone is plugged in to its charger and resting on the pillow beside me. I touch its screen; there are no new notifications. No response to the message I finally sent to Hattie. I unlock the phone and open our conversation, just to be certain. But sure enough, all I find is this, from 3:22 p.m.:

Me: Hi Hattie. Sorry I haven't been the best at texting back lately. I just wanted to let you know, Eva told me you made it into SAB. Congratulations. I always knew you would and I'm so proud of you. Also, I miss you too. And I hope you had a good Valentine's Day.

I turn the phone over and curl onto my side, pulling my knees up to my chest. Which isn't as comfortable as I thought it would be. I shift onto my stomach, but the pillow is too stiff beneath my turned cheek. I flop onto my back. I try to control my thoughts. I try to count my breaths.

I stare up at the ceiling, waiting for my eyes to adjust in the dark.

Once the shadows have shapes and I can see my surroundings, I slide out from the covers and off the mattress. I stand beside the bed, watching as the snowflakes continue to fall.

And then my arms float up at my sides. Not quite to second position port de bras. But to something close. Something like it. My arms extend straight out from my shoulders. My elbows are rounded; my palms gently cup the air. I feel my arms stretch, my fingertips lengthen, my lungs expand. My chin tilts up, my shoulders roll back, a vertebra pops in my spine as my posture straightens.

What am I doing?

The question breezes through me; I ignore it.

I let everything drop. My chin nearly touches

the dip in my collarbone. My arms sweep past my hips and upward, inward, crossing at the wrists before my chest. I hold this position. In my classes, my teachers always say to let your breath travel through your body, down the length of your limbs. I picture it, and I feel it, a warm buzz in my fingertips. Energy in my toes.

I take two steps toward the window. Each one kicks up as a pointed foot, a développé to tendu. The loose pant legs of my pajamas flap as I move, and I almost feel like I'm growing taller with each step. Like my body is suddenly bigger than I believed it to be.

And now, I'm standing so close to the glass, I can almost see myself in its reflection: the faint curve of my cheek, the straight line of my nose, the dark gleam of my eyes.

My arms overlap and drift above my head, forming a long oval. Fifth position. My abdomen tightens as I reach. My shoulder blades draw together. My wrists feel weightless. I'm staring out, past the streetlamps and the snowflakes, past the hot-cocoa-colored clouds that span the night sky.

Someone shifts. My heart stalls at the sound of movement. I duck and glance over my shoulder, but none of them are awake; Mom has turned in her sleep, the air leaving her lungs in a heavy gust. She settles into the mattress. Burrows into the blanket. Her breathing turns deep and easy again, like the tide dragging across coarse sand.

I consider sneaking back into bed, trying to fall asleep, as I should.

But I turn to the window instead. To my audience of no one.

25

AN EMPTY STOMACH

February 19

The morning light seeps in, and I am somehow awake. I'm sitting in the armchair by the open window, watching the slow turn from indigo to periwinkle dawn to light gray morning. The clouds have thinned. The road is clear and slick; the sidewalks are crusted in snow.

My body feels jittery. Twitchy. The corners of my eyes feel scratchy and dry. And my mind is buzzing. My hands are restless. I grab my phone and check the screen. I lean forward to adjust the pillow at my back. I reach for the remote and turn the TV on. The local news shows that other areas were hit harder by the storm. A reporter stands in a park somewhere, speaking directly to the camera as she gestures to the snowy hillside, the shaggy white trees. A list of school district closures scrolls across the bottom of the screen. Aerial footage shows cars abandoned at the edges of freeways and side streets. Huddled and buried in the whitened landscapes.

Mom stirs. She props herself up on her elbow, squinting in my direction. "Good morning," she says after a pause. Her voice is rough; she clears her throat. "You're awake early."

I nod in response.

"Is everything okay?"

I say, "It snowed."

"*Oh.*" She sits up a little straighter. Smiles at the open window. Her hair is a tangled pouf at the back of her head. "How lovely."

I tell her, "Connor will think so, too."

"Should we wake him up?"

She doesn't wait for my opinion. She slides out of bed; Jack senses the movement in his sleep and rolls into the open space, flinging one arm out across Mom's pillow. Mom crouches at Connor's side of the bed; he's asleep on his stomach, his face turned to the side. She presses a kiss to the top of his head and brushes his bangs back from his face.

"Connor," she whispers. She strokes one hand down from the top of his shoulder to the middle of his back. "Sweetie, look outside."

Connor groans. Shakes his head without opening his eyes.

Mom chuckles. Gives him a gentle nudge. "Connor, it snowed last night."

For a second, he goes perfectly still. Then he snaps upright in bed. "Snow?" He looks out the window and his entire face lights up. "Snow!" He swings back around and throws his arms around Mom's neck, grasping her in a tight hug as she laughs and embraces him back. "Today," he declares, "is going to be an *awesome* day!"

"I couldn't agree more." Mom beams.

My heart feels lighter as I watch Connor scramble out of bed. He really is the human version of a ray of sunshine. I hope he never changes.

I hope he never becomes a human storm cloud. Like me.

We're on our way to the Cape Alava Trail. This drive is much longer than the one we took to

the clam-digging beach, so we're eating breakfast in the car. Connor is making a mess of his
bagel. Globs of cream cheese have smeared on his
booster seat, his pants, and his chin. I've finished
my own bagel, but my stomach is still groaning.
Jack offers me a strip of smoked salmon, but I lie
and say I'm full.

"Are you sure?" He sounds baffled.

"I'm full," I repeat.

"Geez. I always have room for salmon." He takes
a bite of it, tearing the caramelized pink flesh with
his teeth.

Mom and Jack are listening to their political
podcast again. Since my service is too weak to keep
checking for text messages that probably aren't
coming, I have no choice but to listen as they talk
about climate change. About some new expiration
date the scientists have set for the planet. With the
rising sea levels and the superstorms and the wild-
fires. The end of civilization as we know it.

I want to ask if we can listen to something else.
Music. An audiobook. Literally anything other
than this.

But I don't say a word. Because it will come out
snappy. Or wrong-sounding. I will open my mouth,
and my parents will tell me: *This is important*

information, Maisie. Or: *We need to pay attention.* Or: *This is a call to action.* As if I don't understand what's going on. As if I don't care enough.

As if.

26

NURSERY STUMP

February 19

I keep my eyes down, focused on the slick wooden bridge we're crossing. Its planks are dark and gleaming. My fists grip the rails as I inch my way over the trickling creek to the opposite bank. A few clumps of snow cling to the ends of bare branches overhead, and there are glistening white patches of it on the ground, but they're thawing. Thinning into crystallized crusts. The air smells of damp stones and soil.

I make it across the stream and keep following my parents and Connor down the path, deeper into the woods. Closer to the ocean. The ground is soft and marshy, cluttered in the soggy brown muck of decayed leaves, squishy lumps of moss. Everything in this forest is drenched in a cold sweat: the stiff pine needles, the skinny twigs, the leafy ferns. The roughened boulders. The fallen logs with frayed strips of bark.

Eventually, Mom notices the distance between me and the rest of my family. She pauses to wait for me, smiling brightly before she asks, "How are you doing?"

"I'm good," I say, and I try to sound like I mean it.

"Good!"

She resumes walking at my side. Jack and Connor are up ahead, playing an intense round of "I Spy." Jack has spied something green, and Connor seems desperate to figure out what it is:

"That branch?"

"No."

"That bush?"

"Nope."

"This moss?"

"No."

"Is it a leaf?"

"That depends. Which leaf?"

"This one?"

"No."

Mom keeps pace with me. Sticks snap beneath our hiking boots. We sink and stumble through a stretch of claylike mud. We walk with our hands in our pockets, our gazes fixed on the uneven ground before us.

Then she points and says, "Do you see that? That old growth stump?"

I look up. The stump is broad and gnarled and cracked. The color of its wood reminds me of resin. A warm, amber tone. In ballet studios, open trays of crushed resin are usually set aside for the dancers. If your pointe shoes are too slippery or satiny, you can walk over to the trays, step into them, and grind the resin dust into the smooth fabric. It will help you gain traction.

It's what I should have done, on the day of my accident.

"It's called a nursery stump," Mom tells me. "See the tiny little saplings and green sprigs growing out of it? It's become a home for other plants. Pretty cool, huh?"

"Mhm."

We carry on. Mushrooms appear in clusters

along the edges of the trail, with little round caps the same color as eggshells. Some small critter skirts through the undergrowth nearby, rustling through the leaves. The mist seems to thicken in the canopy above us, like the tree trunks are growing directly into the clouds.

"We're getting closer," Mom says. "Can you hear the waves?"

I focus for a moment. And sure enough, I hear them. A rumble like the wind. A steady rush of noise.

"There was a mudslide in this area once," Mom tells me. "A major one. It buried an entire Makah village."

My head snaps up. "What?"

She gestures vaguely toward the sound of the water. "It happened in the 1700s," she says. "This beach was one of our settlements for whaling expeditions. And there were a lot of families here. A lot of lives were lost."

Fear slithers down my spine. I glance around at the seemingly peaceful woods. "What caused it?"

"The earthquake, probably," Mom says. "Around the same time, there was an estimated magnitude nine earthquake in the Pacific Northwest. We didn't have the technology to measure it back then, of course. But we have the stories passed down from generation to generation. And we know that what happened here set off a tsunami in Japan."

"Really? How is that possible? Japan is so far away."

She shrugs. "The ocean has always connected us."

27

PETROGLYPHS

February 19

We reach the beach. And here beyond the tree line, the waves crash and roar. They roll and churn, hurtling over each other, collapsing across the shore. The seawater is gray today, and the horizon is gone, swallowed up by a bright white fog. The breakers seem to roll in from the edge of the world. From nowhere and everywhere, all at once.

"There are a few little islands off the shore here," Mom says. "But in weather like this, it's impossible to see them."

Jack and Connor are still way ahead of us,

laughing and speaking in pirate voices—off on a mission to find some gold in this gray landscape. This beach is peppered with round stones and broken seashells. The sand is dark and smooth and wet, gleaming like sealskin as the water pulls back. Driftwood logs are shoved against the far end of the beach, almost to the tree line. They're clean and massive and bent in gentle angles. They look like the bones of an ancient giant, one that roamed the earth a long time ago.

"Come this way," Mom says. "There's something I want to show you."

I follow her down the shoreline. The rocks slide and crunch beneath our hiking boots. When bits of shell slip in, the sound is like gravel mixed with porcelain. And the waves keep rolling in, folding and foaming and smashing. They topple over sharp boulders that protrude from the shallows. The sea spray flings high through the air, dashes across the rocks. Another wave sweeps in, breaking over the boulders with a clap like thunder. A splattering gust.

I'm being careful with my knee. Placing each step slowly. Cautiously. I feel a twinge just above my kneecap, but it only lasts a second. Not like my other muscle spasms.

As Mom continues to lead the way, I discreetly pull my phone out of my pocket. Check for notifications. Nothing. No service.

I swallow the disappointment and drop the phone back into my pocket.

Mom and I approach a wide boulder, flat on one side with markings etched into it. Shallow grooves drawn into the rock. There are ovals with lines down the middle. A face with pronounced eyebrows, round eyes, a straight little line for its nose, and a circle for its mouth. Its head is attached to a boxy torso, with squiggly open arms. Below one extended arm, in the corner of the rock, there is another face. Or maybe it's a moon. Whatever it is, it's disconnected from the other shapes. A lone circle with a curved nose and eyebrows, flat dark eyes, and an open mouth.

"*Whoa.*" The word rushes out of me. I've never seen anything like this before.

"Incredible, aren't they?" Mom says. "When I was a little girl, and my family still lived out at Neah Bay, this was one of my favorite places to visit. We would drive down here, and my cousins would all want to build sandcastles, or look at the tide pools. Do normal kid things. And I was the random weirdo who wanted to go around and examine every single rock for more drawings. For more messages like this." She laughs a little at herself. Smiles a small, private sort of smile. "Growing up, I wanted to become an archaeologist. Have I ever told you that?"

I look at her and shake my head.

"Well, that was a long time ago, of course," she says. "By the time I was enrolled at The Evergreen State College, I was no longer sure about what I wanted. Then I met your dad while he was stationed at JBLM, and . . ." She trails off. Meets my eyes.

And I look away, because I know the rest of this story. I know that she and my dad were married young. I know Mom got pregnant before his deployment. I know that he was killed in action before my first birthday, and Mom never went back to school, because she had to find another job, and suddenly she was juggling two part-time positions as well as first-time motherhood, and even though she had her mother to help with the babysitting, it was never really enough. She was young and lonely and grieving. It was the hardest time of her life, and having me there only made it harder.

Mom reaches out. She cups my cheek in one warm, gloved hand, and turns me to face her again. And she says, "Dreams change." She says, "Realities change. People change. We all go through it in different ways."

I hold her gaze. She strokes my cheek with her thumb.

Then Connor comes shrieking across the beach, shouting, "Mom! Maisie! Look!"

We turn to him. He's flapping his arms in his bright yellow raincoat. Jack is a few paces behind him, gesturing at the sea. And as Mom and I look out at the water, I realize the wind has picked up. Cold, briny gusts whip my hair behind my shoulders, tug at the sleeves of my jacket, at the little pink pom-pom attached to my beanie. The fog has cleared a bit. The horizon is still hidden, but the mist has pulled farther away from the coastline.

"It's a whale!" Connor says. "We saw a *whale*."

Jack and Connor reach us. The four of us stand together, watching and waiting for the whale to show itself again. For the flash of a tail. Or a sudden spout.

And there it is. A burst of mist. The rolling curve of its back.

We all gasp and cry out. Connor throws his hands up and cheers. We watch the choppy gray waters, waiting for another glimpse, for the possibility of an entire pod. But nothing else happens. The moment passes, and it's just the four of us, surrounded by the rhythm of the sea, the cool blasts of air, the ancient rocks.

28

SEA CLIFFS

February 19

We eat lunch on a driftwood log, facing the ocean. And then we start to hike back the same way we came.

"It's going to be another long drive to Cape Flattery," Jack says as Connor protests over the lack of gold and treasure he's found on this trip so far. "We need to move, in order to make it to the cape while there's still daylight."

And so, I follow my parents and Connor back into the rustling ferns and swaying trees. Up the wet, winding boardwalks and through stretches of mud that cake my hiking boots in sludge. Across the bridge above the Ozette River. And finally, eventually, all the way back to our car.

We drive north for over an hour.

The roads to Neah Bay are long and laced through thick evergreen groves. We curve alongside steep, vertical bluffs. We catch glimpses of the Strait of Juan de Fuca, which is also shrouded in patches of mist. Like tufts of clouds that have somehow become stranded on earth.

And there is more snow here. The tree branches are dusted in white and drooping. Streaks of gray slush have gathered down the middle of the road. Blades of grass poke through the inch-thick blanket of snow on the ground.

We make it to the trailhead at Cape Flattery. Connor is the first to climb out of the car and run up to the bulletin board at the head of the trail. There is a map of the area, some historical and ecological information, an excerpt on the Cape Flattery Lighthouse on Tatoosh Island, and some reminders to be respectful of the wildlife, and to closely supervise young children. There is also a stack of walking sticks propped up beside a handwritten message encouraging visitors to use them. Some of these walking sticks are decorated with beaded strings and feathers.

"Cool!" Connor yells. He takes one and stands it upright; the stick is taller than he is. But he reaches up and touches the pink feather attached to it. "Maisie, do you want this one? You can have it."

"I'm okay, Con."

He looks up at me. "Don't you want to try and use it?"

I shrug. "I'm fine."

"But, Maisie—"

Jack says, "She said no, bud. That's enough."

Connor turns to Mom. "Mommy, do you want this? Could you bring it, in case Maisie changes her mind?"

"Of course, sweetie." Mom takes the walking stick from him, lifts her phone in her other hand, and gestures at the oversized blue chair a little farther down from us. The words "Neah Bay, WA" curve across its top, along with a painting of the lighthouse. "Let's take some family photos before we walk down!" Mom says. "Come on, everyone, real quick."

Connor and I both groan.

"But, Mommy," he whines. "I want to look for *treasure*."

"How about we take pictures on the way back?" Jack asks. "It should be the golden hour by then, anyway. Perfect for photography."

Mom sighs. "Okay," she says. "On the way back. No buts."

We start to move down the sloping trail. Sharp winds cut through the trees, filling the woods with an echoing hush. Branches dance and bob all around us. In the distance, I hear a splintering crack and my head snaps up just in time to see a short branch fall from the canopy, crumpling in the undergrowth below.

We reach narrow wooden staircases that draw us deeper into the forest. Our hiking boots land on the crooked planks with hollow thumps. Mom is lifting her phone, taking pictures of the forest from every possible angle. Connor is still chattering about treasure, and Jack is trying to explain to him that we aren't going to another beach. That we will not reach the water here. And that we absolutely will not leave the designated trails, the boardwalks.

My boot skids slightly on a damp stair. I catch

myself, but the impact tweaks my knee. I feel the muscles around it burn and tighten into a knot as I keep following my family. But I fall back a little bit. Shake it out. Take a deep breath.

It's not that bad; I can get through this. I can push through.

I take another steadying breath. I think of the auditions this spring. The possibility of a summer intensive on the East Coast. And I keep walking, moving forward, the only direction I need to go.

Mom turns to check on me. "How's the knee?" she asks. "We're doing a lot of walking today. Is it too much?"

I tell her, "It's totally fine."

"This is the most physical activity you've had in months," she marvels. "Does it feel nice to be out and about?"

I nod and she grins at me, pleased.

At the bottom of the trail, the boardwalk splits in a few different directions. There are multiple viewpoints from the top of this sea cliff. The crash and roar of the water has been muted to a mumble at this distance, the waves are so far below. The winds whistle and shift all around us.

The fog has rolled even farther back, a clouded

gray wall miles off the shore. There are still tendrils of mist threaded through the evergreens that rise along the surrounding bluffs. But the sky is peeking through the thinning white haze overhead, in pale blue patches. And these flashes of blue have deepened the color of the water to sapphire. Which is fitting, because the small islands here remind me of emeralds in the rough. And the boulders peeking out from the lapping waves remind me of polished onyx.

My knee throbs slightly as I climb the ladder to the main viewpoint. It's a steep, short set of steps leading to a balcony with a wooden guardrail, which overlooks the ocean and Tatoosh Island.

And as I stand in the middle of it, surrounded by the wind and the water and the sky, the swishing briars and hushed fir trees and the conversations my parents and Connor are having, I realize this balcony reminds me of a set piece. From *Romeo and Juliet*.

The balcony.

The thought makes me smile.

I close my eyes and feel the air move around me. That weightless lift of my fingertips. That familiar restless energy in my toes.

"Is Maisie sleeping?" Connor moves closer to me. He pokes me in the side. "Maisie, are you asleep?"

I open my eyes. Bite back the annoyance. "I'm awake, Con."

"Oh. It looked like you were taking a nap."

I turn my back on him. I go down the ladder, ready to go off and find some other quiet place. Some viewpoint where I can be alone.

My feet touch the ground, and I lift my face to the sky, to all those bending branches and drifting clouds. And I'm daydreaming again about returning to the studio. About standing in my sanctuary. That bright, open space. The wide windows. The mirror-lined walls.

And then the impossible happens.

My foot catches on a root. There is a split second of unstoppable momentum. A white-hot *zing* of pain.

And I catch myself too late.

29

END OF THE ROAD II

February 19

I cry out as the pain crumples me. I sense my family in a flurry behind me, Mom's and Jack's voices pitched in panic as I lift my foot and try to hop to the nearest tree trunk to support myself. But the roots jutting out of the ground form a perilous web, and I trip again, catching myself on my hands. Jolting my elbows. The fingers of my fuzzy pink mittens dig into the damp soil, the cold seeping through to my skin.

And the *pain*. How can it be so intense? How is this even possible? One second, barely nudged at the wrong angle, and it's like all my months of physical therapy and recovery and carefulness have been erased. The pain is searing. It empties the air from my lungs. Tears well in my eyes. I gasp and croak. The muscles in my knee throb and tighten to excruciating uselessness.

"*Maisie?*" Jack appears at my side. His arm tightens around my waist, holding me up. His eyes scan my face, my body. "Maisie, what *happened*?"

But I can't speak. I can't form sentences.

My mind is racing, speeding through the hours and days and months ahead, and my heart is pounding, and I can't even bring myself to stop or wipe away the burning tears on my cheeks. A ragged sob rips through me. My right foot is still lifted, dangling helplessly. I swallow a breath and try to hold it behind my sternum as I gingerly tilt and try to put weight on the leg, but I can't. The pain ripples all the way through me. My leg nearly collapses. Bright spots form along the edges of my vision.

Mom is in front of me now, and she's saying, "It's okay, sweetheart." She's saying, "It's okay, keep your weight off of it. Don't press down. Just lift your foot—yes, that's right. That's my girl."

A pathetic mewling sound rises in my throat. Terror grips me by the jaw. My teeth are clenched so tight, I briefly fear they might crack and break. But even that wouldn't be any worse than this.

I've already had the surgery. The surgery that was supposed to fix everything. I've had the surgery, and I've been in physical therapy for months, I've been hitting every milestone. And for what?

How will I ever return from this?

I won't. I won't.

"I need you to put your arm around my shoulders," Jack says. "We're going back to the car now, okay? And I'm going to help you. But I need you to lean on me a little bit. I need you to trust me."

I'm hiccuping sobs. And I'm reaching across his shoulders, accidentally smearing bits of dirt on his black winter jacket. My fuzzy pink mittens are smudged in filth. Probably ruined. Like my knee.

Like me.

Jack helps me hobble a few steps back up the trail. But the roots seem to suddenly be springing up everywhere. Blocking me in. My foot on the ground is cramping, the arch of it burning.

"Here," Jack says, bending to pick me up. "Here, let me carry you."

And I know he's being as careful as he can, but the moment his arm sweeps behind my legs to hoist me up, the pain turns black and twists through me. Leaves me gaping like a fish out of water. Suffocating on oxygen.

"Okay, okay, that didn't work." He sets me down but keeps my arm wrapped around his shoulders. "I'm sorry. I didn't mean to—"

"Take the walking stick," Mom says, thrusting it into my free hand. "There you go. Is that better?"

The walking stick. I take it from her. Lean against it. And through my blurry vision, I blink up ahead, where Connor is standing. Watching me with wide brown eyes. He is covering his ears with his hands. His lower lip is trembling.

"Maisie?" he says. And his voice is smaller, softer than I've ever heard it before.

I hate the fact that I'm the one who made him go quiet like this. That I'm scaring him like this.

"Come on," Jack urges me. "Keep moving. Keep leaning on me. You're going to be okay, Maisie."

My lungs are contracting. Squeezing like fists. Oxygen pulses through my gritted teeth. And I'm starting to feel light-headed. I'm starting to realize I can't slow my breathing down. It's slipping out of my control. Out of me. Out, out, out—

"*Breathe* slowly," Jack says. "Everything is going to be okay. Just breathe."

"No," I manage to croak. Because it's not. Nothing is okay.

Mom and Jack exchange glances. Then Mom swoops in closer, resting a gentle hand on the center of my back.

"Don't say that," Mom whispers.

Another sound rises in my throat. A desperate cry from somewhere deep in my belly. It builds like a tidal wave and crashes over me, through me, ripping the inside of my throat raw. The sheer agony of it. The pain of it rivals the clenched, burning throb in my knee.

All my hard work. Years of my life, convinced I knew exactly what I wanted to do. Convinced that I had found my passion. That if I could only continue to practice, to work hard and pour all my love into it, I would persist. Maybe join a major company. Maybe tour the world's stages. Maybe perform in productions of *Giselle* or *Coppélia* or *Don Quixote*. Maybe become the next Noelani Pantastico.

The first Maisie Cannon.

But it's all over. That much is clear now.

Jack's arm tightens around my waist. He half carries me across the uneven ground, back onto the boardwalk. The slick and slanting wooden planks. My family surrounds me as slowly, painfully, we continue up the trail. Tears and snot stream freely down my face. I try to pause and wipe the mess away, but there's too much of it. And it's too embarrassing, smearing snot across my upper lip and struggling to hold my balance on one foot, while my whole family is watching.

And so, I'm forced to let it flow. The tears run hot down my cheeks, cooling as they drip down my chin. And all I can do is shudder through the pain. Watch as my breath forms small clouds in the air.

And think about everything I should have done differently.

30

AN ETERNITY

February 19

An eternity passes, and we finally make it back to the top of the trail. My arms are tired from supporting myself on the walking stick and Jack's shoulders. It reminds me of the soreness and bruised armpits I used to get from using my crutches.

I'll probably be back on crutches again soon. Mr. Lawson will probably want to see me twice a week, same as before. And he'll probably ask me not to go to the dance school auditions this spring. He'll advise against a summer intensive program. Against me following my dreams.

I can't stop sniffling. My eyes feel red and puffy. The tear tracks down my cheeks have gone cold. Sweaty strands of my hair are stuck to my lips, my face; I can feel them sticking out at odd angles from beneath my pink beanie.

My knee is still uselessly throbbing. Seizing. Aching.

That oversized bright blue chair has come back into view. The one Mom wanted all of us to take a picture with when we first got here. As we carry on toward the car, she doesn't even suggest it, and for some reason, this just upsets me more. Even though I don't want my picture taken right now. The fact that she won't ask bothers me more than I care to admit.

I feel like I'm ruining everything. Like I've been chipping away at this whole vacation. And now I've blown it all to pieces. This midwinter break. Their happiness. My dance career.

All of it.

Mom rushes ahead to open the car door for me. Jack continues to support my weight as we cross the asphalt. I reach for the top of the car and wince as I carefully lower myself to the seat.

Jack's voice is gentle as he asks, "Got it?"

I look straight ahead and nod. I whisper, "Thanks." And I wish I could say more, but that single word snags painfully in my throat.

Connor opens the door across from me, and is about to climb into his booster seat, but Mom stops him. She pats him on the shoulder. Unzips her wallet. Hands him a crisp ten-dollar bill. "Go put this in the donation box by the walking sticks," Mom tells him. "We're going to keep this one for Maisie."

Connor immediately dashes off to deposit the money. Mom opens the trunk to tuck the walking stick away. Jack closes my car door and circles around to the driver's side.

I close my eyes. Focus on breathing.

The rest of my family piles into the car. The doors clap shut. Seat belts click into buckles. I hear the jangle of keys, the flick in the ignition, the awakening gasp of the engine. Then we roll backward, the tires peeling across the wet asphalt, crunching bits of gravel.

Connor is the first to speak: "Does it feel better now, Maisie?"

I exhale. Shake my head. And that small motion seems to shake loose more tears, because suddenly my eyes are filled to the brim again, and I'm whimpering. Sucking in tight little breaths to hold myself together. Trying and failing to feel okay.

Softly, my mother says: "Everything will be okay."

But how can she know that? How could anyone possibly know that?

We don't. We don't.

31

EVEN WORSE

February 19

It's a long and winding drive back to Port Angeles, and Jack takes us straight to the hospital. He pulls up to the drop-off area, and I'm staring at the glowing red letters that spell "EMERGENCY" across the side of the beige building. Short banks of dirty slush are pushed against the edges of the road. It's dark now, just past twilight, and the pain in my knee hasn't dulled at all.

Jack throws the car into park; he and Mom rush to open my car door.

I'm sitting with my ruined pink mittens and

matching beanie in my lap. Both are limp and wet with dirt and sweat. And I know—without looking—that my hair is a mess.

The car door opens. Jack takes one look at the defeated slump of my shoulders and asks, "Can you walk?"

"I don't know," I croak. "It feels even worse right now."

"Can I try carrying you again? Do you think that might help?"

"Maybe."

"Okay," Jack says. "Turn to face me."

I unbuckle my seat belt. Push myself with slow, painful movements, grabbing the seat in front of me for stability. The side of my knee barely brushes the cushion, and it seizes again. The pain rockets through me. Takes my breath away.

"Easy," Jack says gently. "There's no rush."

I'm panting. Gasping for air like I just completed a grand allegro combination. Mom is hovering behind Jack, watching me with concerned brown eyes. Connor is still fiddling with the buckles attached to his booster seat, the straps across his chest; I can tell he wants to get out, to find some way to help. "Mom," he says. "Mommy, I want out. Can I get out, please?"

"Connor, stay put for now. Okay, sweetie?"

"But, Mommy, Maisie needs my *help*—"

"I'm okay, Con," I manage to say through gritted teeth. "Don't worry, I'm—"

I cut myself off with a sharp intake of breath. Jack leans down; he eases his arms around me, and I loop mine around his neck as he lifts me from the car. A high-pitched sound escapes from me as he cradles me in his arms.

He murmurs an apology and tries to shift my weight so that he isn't putting any pressure on my knee. Connor is frantic now, pulling uselessly at the seat belt, kicking his legs out in front of him. "Maisie," he's saying. "*Maisie.* Daddy, wait for me!"

Jack addresses Mom and says, "I've got her. Take Connor and find a parking spot while I get Maisie checked in, okay?"

Mom nods, several times and fast. She presses close, places one hand on my tearstained cheek, and drops a kiss onto my forehead. She says, "I love you." She says, "I love you so much, and we're going to get through this, okay? The doctors will know what to do."

I squeeze my eyes shut.

Jack carries me away, his strides long and brisk as he steps onto the sidewalk. Connor is still calling out, still flailing in the back seat, and I hear the tears in his voice as Mom circles the car and hastily tries to readjust his buckles.

As Jack walks through the automatic doors, I open my eyes and catch a glimpse of Mom climbing behind the wheel. I see Connor's worried face pressed against his window as she pulls away from the curb.

32

HURT PEOPLE HURT PEOPLE

February 19

The ER nurses and doctors who see me say that I'm lucky. They say that the tendon didn't detach again, that it didn't sever or snap like a rubber band pulled too far.

But it is strained. And it will continue to be painful. And I did damage some of the other tendons and ligaments around my knee, so I will need to wear a brace and use crutches again, at least for a little while.

The nurse who filled out my paperwork asked, "How did this happen the first time?"

And Jack answered for me by saying, "Ballet. My daughter is a dance student."

"Oh!" The nurse's face brightened, until she looked at me again and she said: "Oh. Well, I'm so sorry you're going through this."

Ten minutes later, the doctor whisked open the curtain by my hospital bed and said, "So I heard we have a ballerina in today!"

It made me want to disappear and leave my own body behind.

Which is kind of what I did, actually. Because ever since that doctor swooped in, with his grand gestures and his medical language and his coffee breath, I've checked out. I've heard what the adults said as they spoke across my prone body, talking about diagnostic tests and next steps and recovery plans. I was there as they sat me down in a wheelchair and rolled me into the lab for an MRI. I clenched my teeth as they strapped a fitted neoprene brace to my knee, despite how much the pain medication had helped to take away my discomfort.

It was just the sight of the brace. The reality of it. The fact that this was my life, all over again.

And now we're waiting on my discharge paperwork. Jack has gone out to the lobby, to lead Mom and Connor back to this holding area. I think he and Mom didn't want Connor to see me while I was still in excruciating pain, so they kept him away. Which I'm grateful for. Because I didn't want him to see me like this, either.

There is a television monitor mounted to the wall in this room. The volume is muted, and I'm staring at the flickering images. The allergy medicine commercials. The previews for movies coming to theaters this spring. The commercials with smiling families in their bright, gleaming kitchens, wiping spilled juice with paper towels. The side-by-side comparisons of these paper towels, versus some other, more generic towels. How these families keep smiling and laughing, unworried about any potential messes in their lives, because they have these paper towels.

Or something. I don't know. It's all kind of stupid.

Then the show comes back on. And it takes me a moment to realize: this is the show Eva has been begging me to watch. *Catriona's Crown*. It opens with a blonde girl in a burgundy dress, running across a lush green field filled with wildflowers. There is a grand stone castle in the distance behind her, and she is dashing toward the rustic stables. A man with golden hair and bright blue eyes is waiting for her there. He opens his arms for her as she approaches.

This is the moment when Jack pulls the curtain back and my family bursts into the room. Connor immediately rushes to my bedside and throws his arms around my neck, burying his face against my shoulder.

"Maisie," he says. "Are you okay now? Is it still hurting?"

"I'm okay, Con." I clear my throat. Press my cheek against his spiky-soft hair. Meet Mom's gaze as she stands at the foot of the bed.

She smiles, but it's wobbly at the edges. "Ready to get out of here?"

I nod. There's a sudden pang in my chest. Connor seems to sense it; he releases me and steps back. He's staring at me. All three of them are. As if they're waiting for me to speak.

But I have no words.

Jack says, "I scheduled an appointment with Dr. Hart for tomorrow at two. We're checking out of the motel early and taking the ferry back to Seattle around noon."

"Tomorrow?" I glance at Jack. "But we're going to the Elwha River tomorrow."

He shrugs. Stuffs his hands into his pockets. "This is more important."

My breath hitches. I don't know what to say to that. Am I supposed to thank him? Try to convince him not to end this trip early? Tell my family they should go and see the river without me?

I have no idea.

So I pretend to focus on the TV screen.

"What are you watching, Maisie?" Connor asks brightly. He hops up onto the hospital bed and snuggles against my side. I try to ignore how his muddy hiking boots smear the starched white sheets. "Is this a movie?"

I tell him, "It's a show."

"What's it about?"

"I won't really know if you keep distracting me."

"Oh. Sorry."

He goes quiet. Snuggles even closer. Mom and Jack exchange glances, and I can tell they're bothered by my attitude, but neither of them says anything. Instead, they both cross the room and sit on the green pleather chairs pushed up against the wall.

For a moment, we all watch Catriona and Phillipe ride on horseback into the meadow, away from the castle. We let the dramatic orchestra music fill the awkward silence for us.

I wonder what my family is thinking. What they must think of me.

And then Mom pulls her phone out of her pocket. The screen lights up in her hand. She starts tapping and scrolling, her brow furrowed in concentration. And I don't know why, but the fact that she's on her phone right now, the fact that she could stomach social media at a time like this, when her daughter is in the hospital—it makes me so angry. I mean, wow.

"Can you not?" I snap through my despair. "Why do you need to be on your ph-phone right now? Why are you always on your stupid phone?"

Mom glances up, surprised.

Jack narrows his eyes at me. There's a warning in his voice as he says, "Maisie. Don't."

But I stare back at them and say, "It's true." Because it is. My mother practically lives on her phone. She is constantly taking pictures, constantly following hashtags. And it's totally okay for her to do that, but anytime I barely peek at my screen, someone scolds me. Why am I always the one being punished? Why does it feel like I can never get anything right? Why can't anything ever be fair in my life?

Mom says, "I just had to check something—"

"Every minute of your life," I mutter.

Jack says, "That's enough. Show your mother some respect."

"But she doesn't need to respect me?" I ask, chest heaving. "How does that make any sense?"

Jack's eyes pop. "Maisie, how could you even—?"

Mom places one hand on his knee. Gives it a gentle squeeze, silencing him. Connor glances back and forth between me and our parents. I can tell how nervous he is. I feel a pinch of guilt as he fidgets beside me.

"Maisie," Mom says. "Look at me."

I blink. Breathe. Meet her gaze again.

33
MORE THAN WHAT WE GOT

February 19

Mom releases Jack's knee. She clicks her phone screen to black and turns it over and over in her hands. Her gaze drops and she sighs.

"You know," she says, "I hear you. Sometimes I think about how much I rely on this device now. How I use it for everything. Pictures. Messages. Social media. How I have apps for banking, for meditating, for tracking my daily steps, for playing music and podcasts." She looks up at me. Shrugs. "It wasn't always like that. Phones used to just be phones. I remember calling my friends on landlines

when I was your age. I remember going to libraries and internet cafés in order to check my emails
in college. I remember—" She swallows. "I remember buying my first cell phone. A flip phone. It was
this indestructible little brick; no matter how many
times I dropped it, the screen never shattered. And
it had one of the earliest phone cameras, so the
picture quality wasn't too great, but that didn't
matter."

She shakes her head. "It really didn't," she says.
"Because all I wanted was the ability to send your
dad pictures during his deployment. I just wanted
him to be able to see you. The screens were tiny,
the pictures were pixelated, and the phones were
a huge expense for us, but it was worth it. It made
him happy. He felt like he was missing out on so
much. So many firsts with you."

Heat rushes into my cheeks. Shame settles deep
in my belly.

"I heard your father's voice for the last time
through that little phone," she says. "I remember it
so clearly. Our last conversation. I told him about
how it'd been pouring all week, but that day the
rain had stopped long enough to take you out for
an afternoon walk in your stroller. How it felt so

good to get out of the house for a while, breathe some fresh air. I told him about the new onesies I'd bought for you, which were all patterned with polka dots, and tulips, and pink teddy bears. I promised to send pictures to him, after your bath. He laughed and said that your fashion shoot would be the highlight of his whole week."

She draws a shaky breath. Chuckles a little. "He had a great laugh. He was kind of a quiet, serious person. A total perfectionist. But when he laughed? God, it was contagious. It was the best sound." Connor nudges closer; he rests his cheek on my shoulder. Mom looks up at us with a smile and says, "That's when you remind me of him the most, Maisie. When you laugh your deep belly laugh." Her smile fades. She holds my gaze. "But that laughter of yours has been rare lately. I can't even remember the last time I heard it."

I have to look away. It suddenly hurts to breathe.

"Anyway," she says. "I remember telling him to be careful. I always reminded him to be careful. I told him that I loved him, I missed him, and I couldn't wait for him to come home. And he laughed again. He said all the same things back, and he told me not to worry. He promised to call again as soon as he could.

"We hung up, and I went about my night. Gave you your bath. I took pictures of you in the new onesies, before I put you to bed. Sent them along to him, as promised.

"But he never responded. I checked my phone the next morning, and he hadn't said anything about your pictures, hadn't given me any updates about where he was or how things went the day before. Which wasn't too unusual. He couldn't carry his phone around while he was in the field, and there could be days—or even weeks—when I wouldn't hear from him. And he wasn't always able to update me on where he was going, or how long he'd be offline. I tried not to worry about it too much. I trusted that I would hear from him, when his mission was over. As I always did.

"Four days later, the army officers knocked at my front door." She stops. Runs one hand roughly down her face. "This is the part I don't remember so well. I know they were dressed sharp in their formal uniforms. I know that they asked if they could come inside. They told me I should sit down. When the news came, I screamed. I yelled at them. In the moment, I think I *blamed* them. I can't recall everything I said, but I'm fairly certain I told them it was their fault, that they took him away from me, from his family. I hit one of the men square in the chest, and slapped him across the face, before I collapsed in a heap on the floor."

The room goes completely still. Jack and Connor and I don't breathe for a long moment. Mom's face is turned toward me, but her eyes are unfocused. Her skin is pale.

I've never heard this story. I've never known her to be violent toward anyone.

"I have no idea how long those officers were in my house," she says. "But I know they didn't leave me alone through that initial, horrific wave of grief. One of them—the man I hit, I think—sat me down on the couch and let me sob against his shoulder, maybe for an entire hour. And by some small miracle, you weren't there to witness any of this, Maisie. At least not at first. My parents were watching you. They had taken you to their apartment so I could get some cleaning done around the house." She shifts her weight on the bench. Rolls her shoulders. "Needless to say, I didn't finish cleaning."

Another breathless silence. Mom seems to blink a few times and comes back to herself, her eyes focusing on me again. Jack quietly wraps one arm around her. Connor makes a soft sniffling sound.

Her voice is ragged as she says, "The first protests I ever attended were against endless wars in the Middle East. Did you know that? I was a senior in high school, and I took the bus all the way from Tacoma to Seattle, to march with everyone who thought the best way to support our troops was to save them. I remember walking through the streets downtown with tens of thousands of other people and thinking, *Wow, we might really be able to stop this from happening.* But we didn't stop anything, did we? And who paid the price? Who lost the most?"

At her pause, I whisper, "Lots of people. Innocent people."

"That's right," she says. "An entire new generation of refugees. An entire new generation of orphaned children. Too much trauma. Far too many tragedies. And for what?"

Jack sighs. Sweeps his hand across her back.

"And your dad was gone," she says. "The man I loved. We were supposed to have a lifetime. We were supposed to have so much more than what we got. And I was filled with guilt and anger and sorrow. I was afraid for the future, and I regretted the past. I kept thinking: if only we'd done more to stop the war. If only we'd done more than march and petition, if only we'd found some other way to stop it all from happening. And when I realized this was irrational, I started to wish for other things: if only he had been stationed in some other place. If only he could have seen those pictures of you, before he left for that mission. If only his tribe had won state recognition years ago, then maybe he would've gone straight to college, instead of enlisting in the military at all. I kept imagining these impossible scenarios where something was different, where some small detail could have changed the outcome of our story.

"I won't lie to you, Maisie. It took me a long time to stop feeling those regrets. It took me a long time to realize that there was nothing I could've done. No way to ever bring him back. And that I couldn't spend the rest of my life chasing his ghost, wishing for a life other than the one I was living."

I blink back the moisture in my eyes and stare up at the white ceiling tiles.

And I ask her, "How?" Because it occurs to me that I've never really asked this. How did she find the strength to move on? How does she keep going? Even after everything.

"Well," she says. "I turned to the teachings of my ancestors, for one thing. I looked back at our histories of resilience and survival. How the Makahs managed to bring their community together, despite horrible events, like that mudslide I told you about. And I spent a lot of time with my family. I focused my energy on you. Raising you. Being there for you when you needed me." I hear the smile in her voice as she says, "And also, therapy. I had a really great therapist."

I glance at Mom. Her eyes shine as she looks back at me.

"In fact," she says, "that's why I was on my phone. I was about to shoot her an email. I want to see if she works with children. And if she does, I'm going to ask if she'd be open to seeing you."

34

THIS LOSS

February 19

There is a short, stunned silence. Or at least, the silence feels stunned to me. Maybe not to Mom and Jack, who are both observing me with expectant looks on their faces. Maybe not to Connor, who is still nestled against my side.

My throat is scratchy as I say, "A therapist?"

Mom nods.

"But I already have one."

"You have a physical therapist," Mom says. "But you don't have someone to talk to, about this moment in your life. The crossroads you're standing in right now."

"You're not making any sense."

"Sweetheart, Jack and I have already discussed this. We think you need to confide in a professional. We think you need some guidance. Someone who can help you sort through these feelings, this—this loss you're going through . . ." She trails off. Looks at me with pleading eyes.

"This loss," I repeat in a whisper. "So you think it's over, then? My time in ballet?"

"We wouldn't have said so," Jack murmurs. "But that's what you told us, in the forest. You repeated it over and over."

Did I?

I can't even remember. I know I thought it; I didn't realize I'd said it.

"For what it's worth," Mom says gently, "I think this is the right choice. I think your body needs to recover. And I think this is a great time for you to focus on your other interests. Maybe even find a new passion."

"Or, you know, you can just enjoy being a *kid*," Jack says. "I mean, really."

"Very true," Mom agrees.

"But—" I attempt to clear my throat; it doesn't work. "But am I giving up? Isn't quitting kind of the same thing as failing?"

"None of this means that you've failed," Jack tells me. "It just means that you're moving forward. Which is about the bravest thing any of us can do."

My voice still sounds thick as I say, "But all of my friends are from ballet. All of them. I don't h-have anyone in my middle school."

Mom sighs. "Oh, Maisie. I know how hard it is to feel far away from your friends. But luckily for your generation, distance doesn't equal the end of friendships. At least, not like it used to. These days you all have phones. You can call or text each other anytime. And when you're old enough, you'll probably find each other on social media. And there are so many other ways to stay connected; it doesn't have to be digital. But that's one way in which technologies have helped us, isn't it? I mean, I'm always chatting with friends from high school and college online. I'm always seeing pictures from your dad's side of the family, even though none of us have physically seen each other in years. It's all so possible now. And besides, you can always find and make new friends. People who share your interests outside of ballet."

"But I'm not like *you*, Mom. I can't just—I'm not always—" I squeeze my hands into fists, frustrated with myself. "My friends do text me. But I don't always message them back. I don't always know what to say. Sometimes texting or talking just makes me so tired. You probably don't even get how something like that can be hard. But it is. It's hard for me."

Tears sting the corners of my eyes. I wipe them away with my sleeve.

Connor pats my uninjured knee.

"And I—" I choke down a sob. Gulp the air. "I love ballet. I love dancing so much. I can't imagine what my life would be like without—without—"

With these words, I can't really hold it together anymore. I'm sick and tired of pretending to be strong. I'm sick and tired of pretending, period. And as I start to cry, the realizations start to hit me, all over again. They're raw and real, like a reopened wound.

I started ballet lessons when I was four years old. And at first, it was all just fun and games. I remember skipping across the studio floors, spinning with colorful scarves in my hands. I remember the teachers telling us to hold our arms rounded, like we were carrying imaginary beach balls.

I remember growing older, growing taller,

growing stronger, all while attending ballet. How I met my friends in the studio. How I started attending auditions and working hard through rehearsals. That soaring sensation in my heart, after every perfectly executed combination, after every onstage performance.

Can I live without all of that?

Can I really?

"Take it from someone who has gone through big changes, someone who's experienced the loss of love," Mom says. "It will hurt. Making your way through these crossroads will be painful and scary and unpredictable. There will be times when it will feel like the hardest thing you'll ever have to do. And there will be times when you feel unsure of your ability to handle it." She leans forward on her elbows. Looks me in the eyes. "But you can. And you will. Because you must."

Connor nestles more firmly against my side. He continues to pat my uninjured knee as I sniffle and shake my head.

"I'm not like you," I tell her again.

"You're very much like me," she says. "I cried and threw a fit when my parents decided to move us away from Neah Bay. In the first full year at my new school in Tacoma, I sat alone at lunch. I felt far away from my friends, my extended family, from everyone and everything that I loved. And it felt like the end of the world, but it wasn't. I grew up and grew stronger from the experience, and I learned to fight for what I believe in. Learned to stand tall. Learned to love my people harder. And then I lost your father, and it felt like the end of the world all over again. But it wasn't. It was tragic and horrific, and I still carry so much love and sadness for him, but it's a weight I've learned to bear. And luckily for all of us, I was able to move forward. I took a chance and was open to falling in love again."

Jack gives her an affectionate nudge. "Thank God for that," he says. "Because if you hadn't, Connor wouldn't be here. And imagine how boring this world would be without him."

Connor goes wide-eyed. "What?"

Mom smirks at Jack. Turns her attention back to me. She bites her lip and says, "But I had a lot of help. And I want you to feel supported too, Maisie. So what do you think? Would you be willing to see a therapist? Someone who could help talk you through these feelings?"

There is a heavy feeling in my chest. Connor looks up at me, his warm brown eyes fringed by his long eyelashes. Jack gives a slight nod when I look at him; Mom watches me with a hopeful expression.

"Okay," I murmur. I still don't think that talking to a therapist will change anything.

But I'll go. I'll try. For them.

35

I'LL BE OKAY

February 19

On-screen, Catriona says: *"Phillipe, I don't care about my family's status anymore. I don't care if they think you're wrong for me. They can keep my crown. All I want is to be with you!"*

We're still waiting on my discharge paperwork, and the episode is nearly over. We've been quiet for a while now; our conversation was intense and tiring. This whole day has been exhausting; I can barely keep my eyes open.

Phillipe says: *"You can't do this. I won't let you sacrifice your future for me."*

Catriona says: *"It's my choice. I choose you!"*

"Do you really think you can live happily as a peasant? You've never known hunger, Catriona. You've never known what it's like to want things you can't have."

"If you truly believe that, then you haven't paid attention to a word I've said!"

Phillipe huffs in frustration, takes her face in both hands, and kisses her on the mouth. Connor yelps and covers his eyes, blasting me in the ribs with his elbow, making me wince.

"Ick." His face is puckered like he's eaten something sour. He peeks at the TV through his fingers. "I didn't think this was a kissing show. Why does there have to be kissing?"

My phone starts buzzing loudly in the pocket of my red coat, which is slung across Mom's lap. It must be Eva, freaking out over that kiss.

My throat tightens as I think of Eva. Of her not knowing where I am. Not knowing what happened to me at all.

A new nurse breezes past the curtain with a clipboard clutched in his hands. He smiles and introduces himself, explains that he is stepping in while our previous nurse clocks out for the night, and hands the paperwork over to my parents.

"I need you to initial here and here, then sign

and date here," he says, indicating the open lines. Mom balances the clipboard on her knee and reads through the fine print, her lips moving soundlessly. She gives a slight nod and scribbles with the pen he offers to her.

"Great," the nurse says. "I'll be right back with a wheelchair."

He leaves, and my phone buzzes again inside the jacket. Mom pats it and nods at me. "Want to check this? It seems important."

"Later," I tell her.

She says, "Okay," even though her eyes look worried.

We watch as the scene on TV changes from the happy couple in the wildflower meadows and sunshine to the dark, dreary cellars in the castle's dungeons. A cloaked figure is hunched over a worktable filled with bubbling cauldrons, vials of neon-colored liquid, and candles dripping wax.

"Aha," the mysterious potion brewer says, lifting a vial of blue fluid in one hand. *"At last. The perfect poison elixir, just as His Royal Highness requested."*

Connor gasps. The episode ends, cutting immediately to a short preview of next week's episode.

"Poison?" Jack says in distress. "Is Catriona's

father trying to poison Phillipe? Would he really do that?"

Mom pats his knee. "You'll have to watch it next week to find out." Then she stands, drops my red coat into Jack's lap, and says, "Connor, why don't we bring the car around, so Maisie doesn't have to go through the entire parking lot?"

Connor says, "I want to stay with Maisie."

"Go with your mother," Jack tells him firmly.

"But, Daddy—"

"No arguing. Just do as you're told, please. It's been a long day."

"That's right," Mom agrees. "We all need to get back to the motel, and we need to rest. Come on, Connor."

"*No*," Connor says, his voice rising to a higher pitch. "I'm staying *right here*."

"Maisie will be right behind us—"

"Mommy, I already said *no*."

I give him a gentle nudge. "It's okay, Con. You should go with Mom. Hold her hand in the parking lot, and look both ways when you're going across the crosswalks, okay?"

"But, Maisie, I can't leave you. I can't." His chin wobbles as he speaks. He stares at me with wide, earnest eyes.

"You're not leaving me," I tell him. "You're just making it easier for me. I'll see you in less than five minutes."

He looks uncertain.

"I'm serious, Con. I'll be okay."

"Are you sure?"

I swallow. "Positive."

He still isn't totally convinced, I can tell. But I stare back at him with a look that I hope is reassuring. And it must be, because he launches forward, wrapping his arms around my torso in a rib-crushing hug. I place my hands on his back. Stroke his shoulder blades. His bones are pointy and pronounced, even through his multiple layers of clothing.

Then he releases me. He hops down from the hospital bed, his muddy hiking boots hitting the glossy floor below. He goes to our mother and takes her outstretched hand.

She smiles at me. "We'll see you in the car."

I nod, and they slip through the curtain, out into the bright, bustling halls of the hospital.

36

SOMETHING I NEED TO SAY

February 19

As we sit and wait for the wheelchair, Jack watches the TV, and I watch Jack. In this fluorescent lighting, the blemishes and wrinkles in his brown skin look more obvious than usual. There is a crease between his eyebrows and crow's-feet around his eyes as he squints at the TV screen. His short black hair is peppered with silver strands. His posture sags, his shoulders are rounded. He looks so tired and unlike his usual vibrant self, worn down after everything that happened today.

Sometimes, I forget that Jack is a few years

older than Mom. And that I've known him for as long as I have. Sometimes, I forget that as I continue to grow older, so does he.

I don't know why this is suddenly hitting me right now. This pang in my chest.

"You know," Jack says, "I've been told many times that I'm eerily beautiful, but even so, it's rude to stare."

He turns to me with a smirk, but the corners of his mouth droop when he sees the look on my face.

"What just happened?" he asks. "Are you okay?"

I nod and sniffle and look away, even though I feel silly and stupid for getting emotional all over again. Out of nowhere. Seriously, what is wrong with me? Who cries this much, other than newborn babies?

"Therapy will help," Jack says gently. "I know you probably feel trapped by your own thoughts and emotions right now. But it won't always be like that."

I nod again, trying to trust him. Trying to believe him.

The program on TV is a show about shipwrecked pirates. They're all stranded on a deserted island, afraid to signal for help from passing ships in the distance, because they could belong to their enemies. To the empire trying to control trade and immigration across the seas.

"We cannot go and blindly seek the empire's aid," the pirate leader says. *"They will likely arrest us before helping us."*

"He's smart," Jack says. "I'm rooting for this guy."

I can tell he's trying to distract me. Trying to lighten the mood.

But there's something I need to say to him. Something that has already gone unsaid for too long.

"Jack?"

He looks at me again. "Yeah?"

It takes me a moment to get the words out. To put them together right in my head. I take a deep breath. Chew nervously at my bottom lip.

"I'm sorry. For the other night. For saying you weren't really my dad. It wasn't the right thing to say, and it isn't how I truly feel."

His eyes soften around the corners. "Maisie—"

"You've always been there for me. And I just wanted to thank you. For today. For everything."

A moment of stillness. Jack is now leaning forward slightly, his elbows propped on his knees as he stares at me. The pirate leader finishes his speech, there's a break in the scene, a cut to the commercials.

And Jack says, "Thank you for the apology. I love you. You're my daughter. No matter what."

I tell him, "I love you, too."

The nurse whisks the curtain open and pushes a wheelchair and a set of crutches into the room with us. He's accompanied by an elderly woman, April, the hospital volunteer who will wheel me safely to our vehicle. April smiles and waves hello. Then the nurse gives us both a smile, wishes me a speedy recovery, and goes on his way to check on his other patients.

Jack helps me move off the hospital bed and into the wheelchair. He tells me to put my jacket on now before we go outside. And as I lean forward in the cramped seat to push my arms through the sleeves, he hovers behind me, chatting with April and holding the coat open for me, in line with my shoulders. I feel the weight of my cell phone in my pocket as I settle in.

From there, April takes over. She pushes me down the bright white hallway, lined with doorways and drawn curtains and hand sanitizer dispensers mounted on the walls. Jack walks briskly at my side. We pass by EMTs pushing gurneys, doctors striding out of elevators, nurses hurrying along in their sky-blue scrubs. The fluorescent bulbs cast spots of bleached light onto the tiled floors. The wheelchair has a squeaky wheel.

We push through the door that leads into the lobby. There are potted plants in every corner of the room, TV screens positioned on the walls, cushiony chairs and couches. Men and women are seated in clusters throughout the space; many of them look tense, worried. The walls are painted in shades of dusty pink and mint green. The wide receptionist desk is made out of a honey-colored wood.

We pass through the automatic sliding doors, and the cold air rushes forward to greet us. It's crisp and clear, and it smells of snow and concrete and pine trees. Thick clouds swirl in the dark sky. Our car is idling by the curb; the engine is rattling, the exhaust pipe emitting fumes in the icy air.

Jack thanks April for her help as he opens the door for me, and Mom waves hello from the front of the car. Connor is already asleep in his booster seat; his chin is tucked against his collarbone, his mouth hanging slightly open.

Mom shrugs and whispers, "I could tell he was tired. That's why I asked him to come with me."

Jack helps me slide from the wheelchair to the

back seat. April waves farewell as she takes the wheelchair and rolls it back inside the hospital. Jack stores the new crutches in the trunk of our car. I close the door as gently as I can, in an effort not to disturb my brother.

Once everyone is in the car, and Mom has verified that we've all buckled our seat belts, we pull away from the curb. We round the corner toward the hospital's exit. We pull up to the short line of cars waiting there, the right-turn blinker ticking into the silence. Out of nowhere, my phone buzzes again. I glance down; the screen is lit up. It looks like a fallen star trapped inside my pocket.

There are fifteen unread messages. Eleven are from Eva (and a quick scroll confirms they are all directly related to that kiss, as well as the poison), and the other four are from Hattie. My heart flutters as I open hers first.

Hattie: Maisie! I'm so happy to hear from you. Sorry I didn't answer right away, Mom and I were on a plane to Florida. We just left the airport, and we're on our way to the hotel in Miami now.

Hattie: Thank you for your kind words about SAB. I'm really excited. The only thing that would make this news better would be if you were going with me. How's the knee? Any updates?

The third message is a photo of the beach: a long stretch of white sand, a cloudless blue sky, and a glittering turquoise sea. The caption reads: My view right now.

Her fourth message is the one that just came through a few seconds ago. It says, Hello? Are you there? Please don't shut me out again.

My throat feels achy as I read her words. I clutch the phone in both hands and press it against my chest, hugging it as I try to blink the blurriness out of my eyes. There's so much I have to tell her. So many things I need to share. So many explanations and apologies to give.

I suck in a sharp breath. Search for the courage inside myself to open up, to tell her how I'm really doing. To tell her how I've been these past few months. It's been hard for me to find the words. It's been hard for me to find the motivation to talk with anyone about this heavy feeling in my chest.

But if I'm going to see a therapist soon, I might as well start trying.

I pull the phone away from my chest. And I start to type.

37

ANOTHER SANCTUARY

Four Months Later

Golden bars of light slant through the library's windows. The colorful laminated spines along the shelves shine white with the glare, making me squint as I push my cart of books down the aisle. The library is filled with hushed sounds—clacking keyboards, turning pages, whispers. The air in here smells of ink and paper.

I find the gaps I'm looking for and return the titles to their rightful places. I bend carefully as I tuck the books into the bottom shelves. My knee is feeling okay today; there's a slight twinge as I lower myself, but I breathe through it. My movements are slow and careful.

I rise again and push the empty cart back down the aisle, the wheels squeaking across the carpet. The intercom clicks on: a robotic female voice announces that the library will close in ten minutes. I circle around the bank of desktop computers and inch past the end tables stocked with titles recommended for Pride Month. I swerve around the long wooden tables, where groups of college students are reading textbooks, writing flash cards, typing on their laptops. I pass by the reading corner in the children's section, where two brothers have pulled an entire stack of picture books from their shelves.

Four months ago, I started seeing Dr. Estrada. At our first appointment, I entered her office on crutches, with bruises all over my heart. Mom was being relentlessly optimistic, and Connor had come along in the car with us because Jack was working and Mrs. Baransky was out of town. Connor was talking nonstop, telling me all about jellyfish, because his class had gone on a field trip to the aquarium, and the moon jellies were his favorites.

And we were late, of course. We were late, and everything was hectic, and I didn't want to be there.

I didn't want to be anywhere, really.

But there I was. Mom wished me luck as I followed Dr. Estrada into the back room. Connor promised to tell me more about the moon jellies as soon as I returned.

That first session of therapy left me feeling raw and overwhelmed. It was hard to meet someone for the first time and immediately start talking about my secrets, my dreams, my disappointments. All the deepest and darkest and most tender parts of myself.

It was hard the following week, too. Therapy is a lot of work. It might sound like you're just sitting and talking with someone for an hour, but there's more to it than that. She leads me through exercises and gives me homework assignments. She listens to me speak, and she offers good advice. She guides me through my feelings. Through the emotions I don't always have words for.

Going to therapy made me realize my thoughts were like scribbles—like a messy black cloud of lines drawn all over a clean sheet of paper. Working with Dr. Estrada helps me detangle all those lines. It helps me make sense of the chaos in my own heart, my own mind.

During one of my sessions with Dr. Estrada, she

suggested that I join a club, or start doing volunteer work. She wanted me to fill my schedule outside of school, to participate in activities, other than visiting her and Mr. Lawson for therapy. Activities that were easy, or creative, or fun, or social. Activities that gave me something to look forward to. Her only recommendation was to avoid athletics, since my knee is still recovering.

And so, I became a volunteer at the local public library.

I push the empty cart all the way back to the front desk, where Brenna and Ethan are waiting for me. Ethan goes to my middle school; Brenna goes somewhere else in our district. They're the other two student volunteers who come here on Thursdays to help the librarians process returned materials, reshelve books, and sharpen pencils. We also help out on Reading Buddy Nights, when little kids come to the library to read stories with middle schoolers like us. Connor and his friends participate in those sometimes. He usually joins Ethan's reading group, because he's kind of a traitor.

"Maisie!" Ethan shout-whispers, waving me over. "Maisie, come look at this."

I push the cart beside the desk and join them at the counter. They're looking through the new guide for the library's summer reading programs. Ethan flips his sandy blond hair out of his eyes and passes the stapled pages to me. They're still warm from the printer. Brenna scoots beside me and throws her arm around my shoulders.

"Look at the grand prizes," she says. "Tickets to the zoo! And the water park! Even if none of us win the reading log competition, can we make a pact to do stuff like this over the summer?"

Ethan scoffs, "Duh, of course we can."

"Awesome." Brenna bounces on her heels. "The parks and rec guide just came out, too! The new pool is opening on July first, and we all *need* to be there. They're also doing all kinds of free concerts and movies in the parks and stuff. This summer is going to be amazing!"

Ethan and Brenna continue to go back and forth as I turn my attention to the brightly colored library guide. Across the top page, there are the words *Summer Reading Programs & Challenges*. The activities are organized by age group and by the dates throughout the summer. Book recommendations are listed in columns down the sides of each page.

It's going to be a different kind of summer. My first summer without any ballet classes. My first summer after the injury. I feel a familiar pang in my chest as I think about Eva, who's going to a ballet program in Chicago. And Hattie, who's going all the way to New York City. A part of me still wishes I could be doing the things they're doing. A part of me still wishes that I could return to dancing.

And maybe I will, someday. But right now, I need to stay focused on recovering.

And I need to stay focused on reading, if I want to win those tickets to the zoo.

"Maisie?" Brenna nudges me. "You okay?"

I give a quick nod. "Yeah. Sorry. I was just thinking."

"About what?" Ethan asks.

"How much everything changes, I guess."

"Huh." He tilts his head. "But change is good, right?"

"Yeah, change is good."

Someone clears their throat behind us, a patron who wants to check out their books using the self-checkout scanner we're currently blocking. We all murmur hasty apologies and scoot farther down the counter.

One of the librarians—a woman named Birdie, who has blue streaks in her hair, square-rimmed black glasses, and tattoos of red roses down the length of her arms—looks up from her computer monitor. She adjusts her glasses and asks, "All finished reshelving in the nonfiction section?"

We nod.

"Wonderful. Just wait in here for your parents to come get you, okay?"

Ethan flips his hair out of his eyes again and says, "I actually rode my bike here today. It's super nice out."

"Me too," Brenna says. "Except I brought my scooter."

Birdie chews her bottom lip. "Okay," she says. "You two go ahead. Be careful crossing the streets."

"We will," Brenna promises. She turns to me. "Once your doctor says it's okay, you'll be able to ride with us!"

"Yeah." I grin at them both. "That'll be fun."

"Remember to meet me at lunch tomorrow so we can sign each other's yearbooks," Ethan says. He pumps his fist in the air and adds, "Last day of school!"

"Last day of school!" Brenna and I chime back, giggling.

I wave goodbye as they head out the door.

38
CHANGE IS GOOD

A Few Minutes Later

The robotic female voice clicks on again: the library will close in five minutes. Throughout the library, backpacks are zipped shut, people stretch their arms above their heads as they rise from the computer desks, and those two boys from the children's books corner are following their mother to the checkout stand with stacks of picture books in their arms. The younger brother is hurrying to keep up, even though his shoelace is untied.

I wander over to the front shelves. This is where the library's new arrivals are put on display, the freshly laminated hardcovers facing out; they stand tall on their top shelves, their pages crisp and unread, their bindings flexible yet strong.

And just below this display, there are several crowded rows of used books for sale. I run my fingertips along the creased, weathered spines. Some of these paperbacks have been through a lot: pages tinted brown from coffee spills, dog-eared corners, highlighted paragraphs and pencil markings in the margins. Some of their covers are torn. Some were published way before I was even born.

And yet, they're still here. Waiting to share their stories.

I pluck one of the novels from the shelf and fan its yellowed pages open. The book's spine bends easily in my grasp, folding over itself. I breathe the scents buried inside this book: aged paper, and a hint of spice. Something like nutmeg.

"Maisie!"

I turn toward Mom's voice. She's walking briskly, dressed in distressed jeans and a white T-shirt, her black leather purse slung over one shoulder. She got a new haircut recently; she has blunt bangs and long layers now. Her smile is light-bulb bright, and she gives me an excited little wave as she draws closer.

"Hey, sweetie. Ready to go?"

"Yep." I give her a one-armed hug and return the book to its spot on the shelf.

"I heard back from your auntie Alice," Mom tells me. "Her flight is officially booked for next month. She's going to stay with us for a whole week."

"Awesome!"

"I know! She's so excited to see you. She hasn't made it out here since—oh, gosh. Since just before Connor was born?"

"Too long," I say.

"Way too long," Mom agrees.

I've been talking with my dad's side of the family a lot lately. Dr. Estrada thought this was a great idea. She's always telling me to acknowledge my support systems; to reach out to them, and express gratitude to them.

Auntie Alice and I have grown pretty close, for two people who live on opposite sides of the country. We talk on the phone at least once a week, and she texts me funny memes from the internet, or sentimental quotes about the importance of family.

She also agrees with my mom. She thinks I have my dad's laugh.

"What's for dinner tonight?" I ask as we follow the crowd exiting the library.

"Ugh," Mom says as she waves at Birdie. "I'm exhausted from work. And Jack didn't make it home early enough to cook anything, either, so we were thinking pizza. How does that sound?"

"Sounds good to me."

I pause. On the wall beside the double doors, there is a bulletin board. Members of the community can add stuff to it, as long as they ask the librarians first. There are advertisements for local children's theater productions, babysitting jobs, rooms available for rent, the new parks and recreation guide that Brenna mentioned, and a poster of Noelani Pantastico in a simple black leotard, for a recent Pacific Northwest Ballet production called *Director's Choice.*

In the left corner of the bulletin board, there is a new flyer with the headline *The World Is Your Oyster!* In a slightly smaller font beneath these words, it says: *Join our new group for young activists, get involved with local politics, and create the change you wish to see!* There are several more lines of text, describing some of the issues this group has fought for. And there are photos of them doing stuff in the world: cleaning the litter in Carkeek Park, volunteering in a soup kitchen, marching with picket signs at the capitol building in Olympia.

Mom follows my gaze and says, "I've heard of this new coalition. They're doing some great work."

"Really?"

"Really. Kids of all ages can get involved. And look," she says, pointing at the fine print. "They're having a meeting at this library in two weeks."

"Huh." I chew my bottom lip. "Maybe I should go. See what it's all about."

Mom grins. "I think that would be great, Maisie. You're going to have so much free time, once school is out tomorrow. And after we come back from our little weekend trip, of course."

"Yeah," I say. "Totally."

She throws her arm around my shoulders and hugs me tight against her side as we continue on our way out the door.

39
ONWARD

The Last Day of School

Just before the bell rings, I slip into homeroom and hurry to my seat. The air in here smells of sunscreen and body spray. Everyone is restless and chatting, signing one another's yearbooks, paper airplanes soaring through the back rows, cell phones buzzing on tabletops. The bell shrieks, and no one seems to notice.

I drop into my chair. I'm dressed in denim shorts and a red T-shirt, and the smooth metal surfaces are a cool shock against my exposed skin. Goose bumps rise along my arms as I settle in and place my book bag on the floor.

Ms. Porter moves to the front of the classroom and claps her hands to get our attention. It takes a few moments for my classmates to quiet down, for the restlessness to turn to stillness.

Ms. Porter grins and says, "Good morning, students. Today marks the end of our journey together. Take a moment to respond to this prompt in your journals, and then we will end a few minutes early to sign yearbooks and say our farewells. Okay?"

There are murmurs and nods. Someone coughs into their elbow. Notebooks are pulled out of backpacks.

I flip through mine to one of the few open pages at the end. Then I squint at the whiteboard, reading the prompt.

Onward
In a continuing forward direction; ahead.
Forward in time; toward a point lying ahead
    in space or time.
Going farther rather than coming to an end
    or halt.
Synonyms: ahead, forth, forward, on.

My long dark hair spills over my shoulder, brushing the side of my face as I lean forward.

Onward.

I take my time committing this word to paper. I shape each letter with care; I try to space it out all evenly. I draw a slow, wavy line beneath it as I try to figure out how to start this final entry.

And I write: *I don't really know what my future holds.* I swallow. Add another line: *But that doesn't scare me as much as it used to.*

From there, I start to write about my sessions with Dr. Estrada. How she explained that I was showing symptoms of anxiety and depression. How she has helped me work through these symptoms, to feel more like myself again. To feel more present in my own body. To resist that hollow ache that sometimes tricks me into thinking I don't matter. Tricks me into thinking I'm a failure. That I will always be a failure. That I'm *only* a failure. Or that my family doesn't love me as much as I love them. Or that my friends don't really want to hear from me.

Dr. Estrada helped me see that these negative thoughts were nothing more than that. They were just thoughts. Chemical imbalances in my brain.

I draw a sharp breath. Roll my shoulders.

And then, to lighten things up a bit, I start a new paragraph. And I begin writing about all the great things that might happen in my future. All the possibilities that excite me. Because who knows what could happen? Now that I really am feeling better, now that I feel motivated to get out and do things.

Maybe this summer, I'll become well enough to ride my bike with Ethan and Brenna. Maybe I'll get involved with that activist group from the flyer; Mom and Jack would love that. Maybe next year, I'll have even more friends to sit with during lunch. Maybe I'll be placed in a creative writing class, my top choice for an elective course. Maybe I'll go watch another ballet with Hattie and her mom, just like when we went to see *Romeo and Juliet*. Maybe Eva and I can have a sleepover sometime, to watch the first season of *Catriona's Crown*. Maybe someday, I'll become a writer.

I just don't know. And not knowing things can be exciting.

"Okay, students!" Ms. Porter calls out, clapping her hands together. "Let's stop there. I had such a wonderful year with you all. It has been an honor to watch you grow, and I wish you all the best in eighth grade. Feel free to move around and sign each other's yearbooks until the bell rings."

The room promptly breaks into chaos. A few

students call out their gratitude to Ms. Porter, and everyone is suddenly in motion, laughing with their friends, uncapping markers to write in each other's yearbooks. I slide my notebook back into my book bag, retrieve the heavy yearbook, and go to the front of the classroom.

Ms. Porter beams at me from the seat at her desk. "Maisie Cannon!" she says. "Just the girl I was hoping to see. How are you doing?"

"I'm good," I murmur. "Will you sign my yearbook?"

"Of course." She flips through to the staff pages in the back. Starts to pen a message in red ink into the margins by her picture. I politely look away, admiring the potted plants lined up along the edge of her desk. She has a collection of spiky cactuses, mint-green succulents, and orchids.

She finishes her message. Fans her hand above the page to avoid smudging the letters. Then she carefully closes the yearbook and hands it back to me.

"I'll see you in the fall," she says with a bright smile. "Have a great summer, Maisie. I'm still rooting for you."

"Thanks, ma'am. You too."

I carry the yearbook back to my desk. In the short amount of time we've been here, the angle of sun has already changed through the east-facing windows. There is a gleaming puddle of sunlight across the surface of my desk. I set the yearbook down on my desk, the sun heating my back as I flip through to the page she signed.

Ms. Porter wrote: *Excited to have you in my creative writing elective next year, Maisie! I look forward to finally reading your words. I already know they will be brilliant.*

And now I'm really smiling. Hope is filling me up. I tuck the yearbook into my book bag and zip it shut.

40

MAYBE SOMEDAY

After the Last Day of School

The final bell rings, and the entire school bursts at the seams.

Normally, I would be on my way to bus 185. But today, I'm meeting my family in the parking lot out front. I exit through the office doors and step into the warm, dizzying sunshine. I lift one hand to my forehead, shielding my eyes from the bright glare. A group of sixth graders races past me on their scooters. Another group of people are waiting to cross the crosswalk. Bees and butterflies zigzag through the air, the trees lining the sidewalk are leafy and full, and the cars throughout the lot are idling and dusted in pollen.

I cross the blacktop, squinting and glancing around myself.

"Maisie!"

I turn toward Jack's voice. He's standing beside the open driver's door, waving both arms above his head to grab my attention.

I hurry in his direction, lifting my bag off my shoulder as I approach. Jack ducks back inside the car. Mom and Connor both turn to me with smiles as I pop the door open and slide in.

"Maisie!" Connor says. "Maisie, look at what happened!" He holds his elbow up for my inspection; a square, peach-colored Band-Aid is pressed against his tanned skin.

I gasp. "Con, are you okay?"

His basketball shorts are smudged with grass stains. His dark hair is all ruffled, and there's a peculiar spot of dirt on the tip of his chin.

"I fell," he announces, as if this is something to be proud of. "During our last-day Field Day. But don't worry," he adds, reaching across the back seat to pat my knee. "It's okay. I got back up again."

"Well. I'm glad you're okay."

"And how was your last day of school, Maisie?" Jack asks, peering at me in the rearview mirror. "No falls, I hope?"

"No falls," I confirm. "But I do have some exciting news."

Connor gasps and bounces and asks, "What? What happened?" Our parents both turn in their seats to look directly at me.

I give them all a sheepish smile. "It's not certain," I say. "But I think Ms. Porter secretly told me that I'm going to be in her creative writing class next year. Just like I wanted. She wrote it in my yearbook."

My family collectively gasps and cheers. Connor starts clapping. Jack grins at me. Mom says, "That's wonderful news, sweetie!"

I nod and duck my head. Peek at my phone screen. There are three unread messages: one from Auntie Alice, one from Eva, and one from Hattie.

I open them with my thumb.

Auntie Alice sent me an animated GIF of kids running free from a school bus, with the caption School's out for summer! Enjoy it! Eva sent me a mirror selfie from the dance supply store in the U District, with a text that says: Getting ready for

Chicago! I'm trying out some good old-fashioned Bloch pointe shoes this time. Let's hope they won't murder my feet like every other brand does. Hattie sent me a picture of the novel in her lap, and the bags of luggage at her feet. Her text says, Waiting to board my flight to NYC. Thanks again for the book rec. ☺

"Maisie!"

I'm smiling as I say, "One second, Con."

I tap out quick responses to all three of them. Jack pulls us away from the parking space, and we join the line of traffic leading to the exit. The cars inch along, and someone up ahead is blaring their horn. Mom starts playing an episode of one of her political podcasts, the familiar intro music flowing through the sedan's speakers. Once I hit send on my final message, I tuck my phone back inside my pocket and turn to my brother.

"Okay, what's up?"

He gives me an excited little grin. "Do you want to hear even more about Field Day? It was so much fun. We had this huge, super-colorful parachute! And a Hula-Hoop contest! And water balloons!"

I nod along as Connor explains every single activity, every single trip and fall. Because he apparently fell a few times. But he got up every single time, and he keeps telling me over and over about how that's the most important thing. And about how he learned that from me.

"I really did, Maisie," he says. "I learn pretty much *everything* from you."

I catch Jack's eye again in the rearview mirror. We share secretive smiles as Connor continues to ramble on and on.

We drive through the crowded, sunny streets of downtown Seattle, and we arrive at the pier just as the Seattle–Bainbridge Island ferry is boarding. A worker directs us onto one of the ramps, and we pull up and squeeze in close to the car in front of us. Jack cuts the engine, and we all climb out.

I trail slightly behind my parents and Connor, who is still obsessed with jellyfish, and is now going on and on about how he hopes we see some floating in the water. And Mom is asking us if we're hungry. And Jack is holding the door to the stairway open for us. He falls in line behind me as we go up the echoing steps and into the main cabin of the ferry.

There's an achy feeling in my throat. A tightness in my chest.

As we move through this ferry with its gleaming floor tiles and its vinyl booths and bolted-down seats, emotions rise up within me, competing for my attention. There's sadness, as I remember how I felt the last time we boarded this boat. The pain in my knee. The heaviness in my heart. There's happiness, as I watch Connor take Mom's hand, as she laughs at something he's said, as Jack walks by my side. I'm so content right now. So excited to be crossing these waters again. To be heading back to the Olympic Peninsula, to finally see the Elwha River.

It feels like we've gotten a second chance. It feels like everything is exactly how it should be right now.

Mom and Connor lead us out onto the blustery, sun-filled deck. My hair whips across my face, and the fabric of my T-shirt tugs and flaps against my torso. The four of us line up along the green-painted railing. The water below is a deep, rippling blue; the sky above is pale and pretty and cloudless. The Seattle skyline looms behind us, all the steel and glass shining like salmon scales in the sunlight. Down at Pier 57, the Great Wheel keeps on spinning.

Jack nudges me with his arm. "How are you doing, Maisie?"

I suck in a breath, surprised by the tears gathering in my eyes. "I'm good," I say, quickly dabbing at my eyes with the back of my wrist. "I'm great, just . . ."

"Feeling a little emotional?"

"A bit, yeah."

He nods, understanding. "Your mother and I kind of figured that this trip might stir up some feelings for you, Maisie. Which is why we got you something."

I blink up at him. "You what?"

Mom clears her throat and reaches into the depths of the tote on her shoulder. She pulls something out and hands it to me.

And the fresh tears come surging back.

Jack chuckles and says, "Well? What do you think?"

Mom says, "After you told us about your desire to take a creative writing class, we thought it was perfect. We hope you like it!"

My parents got me a journal. A brand-new, totally beautiful composition notebook. The artwork on the cover is of a young bronze-skinned girl in a black leotard, standing at the barre in a ballet studio. She looks like she's about to begin a warm-up combination; there is a window by her, filled with golden light, and the reaching, bright green branches of a tree.

It might be the most beautiful image I've ever seen.

I try to swallow the lump in my throat. I tell them, "I love it." I tell them, "I love it so much. Thank you."

I hug the journal against my chest. Mom and Jack both wrap their arms around me. Connor swoops in too, burrowing his way into the group hug.

Then the ferry dislodges from the pier. It's so smooth, so effortless, it takes us all a moment to realize we're moving. We all giggle and break apart. We stand at the green railing and watch our surroundings change together.

And I keep hugging my notebook. I keep looking at my family. And I think of the stories they've told me. Stories of resistance and triumph and joy from our little corner of the world. Stories of loss and tragedy, and how people overcome losses and tragedies. And who knows? Maybe someday, I'll write a story about all of that. Maybe I'll start planting the seeds of it right here in this journal.

It's impossible to know what the future will bring.

But right now, I choose onward. And my family and I are finally going to see the restored Elwha River. I bet the land around it will be green and blooming; I bet the water will be clear and rushing.

I bet it will be beautiful.

AUTHOR'S NOTE

On May 17, 1999, members of the Makah Nation hunted a gray whale. This was not the first time the Makahs hunted a whale, but it was the first time they were filmed by news helicopters. It was the first time their traditions were discussed and debated and sensationalized by the public.

I was six years old when the *Hummingbird* set out into those choppy Pacific waters. When Theron Parker struck the whale with his harpoon, he led his crew of Makah men in prayer as she died. They prayed to thank the whale for offering herself to the Makahs. She was the first one the tribe had hunted in over seventy years; they had stopped exercising this treaty right after non-Native commercial whaling drove gray whales to the brink of extinction. For decades, the Makahs refrained from this ancient tradition, waiting for the whale populations to grow and stabilize again; they only sought permission to resume a limited number of these hunts after gray whales were removed from the endangered species list in 1994.

The female whale's death brought the Makah community together and inspired a festive gathering with tribal citizens from around the world. A potluck in honor of the whale was held at Neah Bay, with prominent leaders from the Northwestern Coast and Coast Salish regions, as well as honored guests from across North America, the Pacific Islands, and Africa. Throughout the feast, these leaders spoke about the importance of pursuing cultural revitalization and protecting treaty rights.

However, despite the celebration and success of this whale hunt, the Makahs soon faced violent opposition. Protestors anchored their boats along the coastlines of Neah Bay. Hundreds of death threats were called in to the Makah tribal offices. Bomb threats were issued to schools on the reservation. One man wrote a letter to the editor of the *Seattle Times*, asking, "I am anxious to know where I may apply for a license to kill Indians. My forefathers helped settle the west and it was their tradition to kill every Redskin they saw. 'The only good Indian was a dead Indian,' they believed. I also want to keep with the faith of my ancestors." In response to this turbulent violence, the National Guard was deployed to Neah Bay to protect the People of the Cape.

Let's circle back to the fact that I was six years old while all of this was happening. I mostly didn't understand it, since I was young and safe in my own little media bubble, which revolved around reruns on the Disney Channel. And because I was raised in the Seattle suburbs, far away from my Native relatives and the tight-knit world of Indian Country.

But here's the thing about bubbles: they pop. It's inevitable.

When I was a graduate student at the University of Washington, my mentor shared some interview footage with me from the first International Salish

Wool Weavers Symposium of 2016. At the time, I was crafting my own thesis on Coast Salish weaving traditions and learning more about our regional histories and cultural traditions. A Suquamish/Makah Elder was among the interviewees. I listened to her speak about her life, soft-voiced and smiling as she recalled fond memories. Her words stayed with me. And as I watched her footage, I remembered the whale hunt and was struck by an unexpected realization:

Even though I wasn't there, and I had been young, and the exact details of this historic event were foggy in my mind, I remembered what that time was like for me. I remembered how it *felt*. I remembered what it was like to be a young girl, overhearing all the noise and chaos and vehemence of the adult world. I remembered what it was like to feel small and confused and frustrated by circumstances I was powerless to change. I remembered how difficult it was to articulate my response to everything that was happening.

As an adult, I learned some of this history in earnest for the first time, and I sat with the memory of my own discomfort and disillusionment. Through this reflective experience, Maisie came to me. Her voice, her experiences, her ancestry.

She was Makah from the very beginning, but her father's Piscataway background came later. It was a question I'd been pondering for months; I knew her father's story, that he had served and died in Afghanistan. But I didn't know where he was from. To me, it made sense that he wouldn't have been from Washington State. Enlistment in the military typically guarantees relocation. I liked the idea of him coming from the East Coast, because tribal nations are often rendered invisible in these territories, and I wanted to push back against those false assumptions. I wanted to remind my readers that Natives were there before this region became known as the Thirteen Colonies. And more important, I wanted to make it clear that Native people *continue* to live there, in modern urban areas. That they never faded into the past, like the textbooks and monuments and historic battleground sites might suggest.

The answer came to me as I flew into Baltimore for a convention. The Piscataway are known as the People Where the Rivers Blend, and as we descended over the landscape, toward the Baltimore/Washington airport, I could see why.

The vast network of rivers and tributaries took my breath away. I was reminded of the Elwha River. And I was reminded of how deeply connected Native people and communities have always been, no matter the physical distance between them.

On the topic of geography, I'd like to discuss some of the settings found within this book.

Astute readers might have noticed the titles of Chapters 13 and 15. In Chapter 13, Maisie and her family cross the Puget Sound on the Seattle–Bainbridge Island ferry. This chapter is titled "Little Crossing-Over Place" for two reasons: First, because this is the name that Duwamish and other Lushootseed speakers historically used, in reference to the modern city of Seattle. Second, prior to the "founding" of the city, this name was also used to describe a specific lagoon, where at least eight longhouses once stood. (Only the ruins of one longhouse remained there when the Denny Party migrated into the area in 1852.) The location originally known and inhabited as the Little Crossing-Over Place is currently known as the Pioneer Square neighborhood of downtown Seattle. And the Seattle Ferry Terminal is located in this exact area.

In Chapter 15, Maisie and her family arrive in Port Angeles. This chapter is titled "Tse-Whit-Zen" (pronounced ch-WHEET-son), which is an Anglicized spelling for an ancient Klallam village located in what is currently known as Port Angeles. In August 2003, ancient artifacts and human remains were unearthed near the base of Ediz Hook after Washington State Department of Transportation workers began construction on a bridge development. The construction halted, and the Lower Elwha Klallam Tribe worked with a team of archaeologists to recover the remains and artifacts. Through this process, Tse-Whit-Zen became the largest pre-European contact site excavated in Washington State. Over 100,000 artifacts were recovered from the area. The earliest confirmed settlement at Tse-Whit-Zen dates back to about 750 B.C.E.—approximately the same time Rome was founded.

There is another significant excavation site located on the Olympic Peninsula. Among archaeologists, the Ozette site is known as "America's Pompeii," probably because the artifacts recovered from the site of the historic mudslide—which Maisie's mother mentions in Chapter 26—were mostly intact and well-preserved. The excavation lasted eleven years, and produced over 55,000 artifacts. All these materials were kept as property of the Makah Nation and held at the Makah Cultural and Research Center in Neah Bay.

Throughout the process of writing this book, I was deeply inspired by the rich histories of these places. But I was also equally inspired by the restoration of the Elwha River. So far, this is the largest dam removal project in history. Prior to the construction of the Elwha and Glines Canyon Dams, several species of trout and salmon had annual runs of about 400,000 fish in the early 1900s. After the dams' construction blocked the Elwha River, these annual runs lowered to about 3,000 total fish per year. This was the main motivation for the Lower Elwha Klallam Tribe's advocacy for the removal of these dams. After both dams were removed in 2014, the entire ecosystem and regional tidelands experienced epic rebounds. The salmon are returning, along with other species of wildlife. The coastline also changed dramatically, as the river moved sediments that had been blocked by the dams for an entire century.

In essence, the river roared back to life after

these dams were removed.

Scientists continue to research and monitor the progress, as revegetation efforts and wildlife tracking continue along the river, led by the Lower Elwha Klallam Tribe and workers from the Olympic National Park. And as these lessons from the river continue to teach us about the resilience of nature and the role humans play in our own environments, I'm eager to see what future generations will work toward and accomplish together.

I bet it will be beautiful.

ACKNOWLEDGMENTS

You are truly a thorough reader, if you're here with me in the Acknowledgments section. And I love that, which is why I'm acknowledging you first, the person currently reading this book from cover to cover: I see you. I appreciate you. I hope you'll find a lucky penny today.

To Rosemary Brosnan: Thank you for guiding me, for believing in me, and for workshopping this book with me from the very beginning. I'm so proud of everything we've accomplished together, and I'm so grateful for the opportunity to keep working with you. You brighten my entire world. You are such a positive, creative force in my life. And I treasure our friendship.

To the folks behind Heartdrum, the shiny new imprint at HarperCollins dedicated to Native stories and storytellers! Woohoo! Cynthia Leitich Smith, you are the type of person and professional that I aspire to be. You do so much for so many people. I am grateful for your kind and generous spirit, as well as your sharp editorial eye and creative feedback. Mvto! Rosemary Brosnan (yes, I'm thanking you twice), and Courtney Stevenson, thanks for everything you do. And as the president and publisher of HarperCollins Children's Books, Suzanne Murphy also deserves heaps of recognition. Suzanne, thank you for helping to create this space for Native writers. I raise my hands to you in gratitude.

I need to give broad but heartfelt thanks to the rest of the HarperCollins family. To the school and library marketing team, as well as the sales, trade marketing, and publicity folks: I am grateful for every opportunity you give me. Thank you for helping my books find their audience. To the production process team: My books quite literally wouldn't exist without you. Thank you for all of your hard work. To the art department: You take my breath away. Catherine San Juan, thank you for your exquisite design work on this book. It is so absurdly beautiful. And to the warehouse workers, mail carriers, and other folks along the way who transport and deliver my books to my readers: Thank you so much.

To Michaela Goade (Tlingit): You bewilder me. This cover resonates with Maisie's story perfectly, and I'm entranced by your attention to detail: the dusting of snow on her clothes, the sheepskin lining of her boots, how the sea is swallowed by a bright white fog. It all feels so potent and meaningful. When I look at this cover, I feel an ache in my heart for Maisie, and yet, there is still endless beauty in her journey and her surroundings. I'm grateful to know you, and I feel so lucky to have your beautiful work paired with mine. Gunalchéesh!

To Suzie Townsend: Thank you for always having my back, for helping me plan and pursue my biggest publishing dreams, and for working so tirelessly on my behalf. You are a marvel. And whenever I start to feel antsy, or overwhelmed, like I'm falling behind on some imaginary schedule I've set for myself—you always remind me that publishing is a marathon, not a sprint. I'm grateful for your realism, your compassion, and your business savvy. I'm also grateful for your friendship and laughter.

To Dani Segelbaum: Thank you for "circling back" and "looping me in" to so many email chains. And thank you for being so patient and understanding with me, when I get busy and neglect my inbox. I hope you know how much I appreciate you, and how reassuring your organized, attentive presence is to me. (I'm sure Suzie will agree!)

And to the other incredible folks at New Leaf Literary and Media, thank you for everything you do for your clients. I truly believe that New Leaf is the best agency in the business. No one can convince me otherwise.

To the folks at Hedgebrook, who hosted me on Whidbey Island for the inaugural "Young Adult Authors Week" residency in December, 2019: Thank you for your radical hospitality, for the delicious foods shared around your farmhouse table, and for preserving the wild beauty of the lands you reside on. Thank you for the land acknowledgment you shared, which recognized the island as Tscha-Kole-Chy, a traditional territory of the Lower Skagit, Swinomish, Suquamish, and Snohomish tribes. I also need to specifically thank Evie Lindbloom, the Hedgebrook librarian, for being so generous with her time and enthusiasm. Nancy

Nordhoff deserves recognition as well, since her vision, philanthropy, and steadfast commitment to raising women's voices are the reasons why Hedgebrook exists. And I need to acknowledge my friends, Linda and David Wilson, who first introduced me to Hedgebrook.

To the Hedgewitches: Sherri L. Smith, Nidhi Chanani, Brandy Colbert, Stacey Lee, Laura Ruby, and Kip Wilson. The week we spent together at Hedgebrook was such a gift. You were some of the first people to hear snippets of Maisie's story, and your kind words boosted my confidence in a story that was very difficult to write. I will always cherish those nights we spent drinking tea in the farmhouse living room, and the days we spent going on nature walks together. Thank you for being there as I wrote the final few chapters of *The Sea in Winter*. And thank you for staying in touch and celebrating my other projects, all these months later. Your friendships continue to inspire and uplift me.

To Traci Sorell: You are a pillar in the Native kid-lit community, and you are also a dear and supportive friend. Thank you for sharing your thoughtful and thorough newsletters, and for being such a bright and delightful person. I'm grateful for all the work you do. And I'm grateful to know you. Wado!

To Hayley Chewins: You are such a dear long-distance friend and writing peer. I cherish our conversations about craft, which always leave me feeling so motivated and energized. I hope we will get the chance to meet in person someday.

Many thanks to the folks behind the Makah Indian Nation, Lower Elwha Klallam Tribe, and Piscataway-Conoy Tribe's websites. You provided so many great resources, including treaty transcripts (which Jack accesses on his phone in Chapter 17), historical timelines, and language recordings ("See-yah" is an English spelling of the Klallam word for grandparent; a recording of this term can be found on the "Human Relations" list of the online Klallam dictionary). I also need to recognize Dr. Joshua L. Reid, who wrote *The Sea is My Country: The Maritime World of the Makahs*, which helped me gain a better understanding of the 1999 whale hunt. And I would like to acknowledge the folks at the Suquamish Museum, who organized an exhibit on the Elwha River restoration project, which inspired me and led me to do more of my own research on this topic.

To the kid-lit gatekeepers: Teachers, parents,

librarians, booksellers, etc. Thank you for supporting me and my work. Thank you for connecting my words with the young readers in your communities. When *I Can Make This Promise* first came out, I didn't expect much. In fact, I didn't expect anything. I was fully prepared to watch Edie fly under the radar, but thanks to your enthusiasm, she took off and soared instead. My quiet, personal little book. I still can't believe it. Thank you, thank you, thank you.

To my young readers: From the outgoing kids who run up to me during school visits, to the shy kids who want to become writers someday, to the kids who ask questions that make me pause and think. You are all so bright and capable and inquisitive. You are the best part of this whole gig. Thank you for everything.

To my friends and family: My parents, my sister, my in-laws, the extended members of my far-reaching family tree, and the dear friends who have grown and changed with me over the years. You already know how much I love and appreciate you all. Regardless of whether or not you read my books. Regardless of whether or not we agree on certain things. No matter what, I am grateful to have you in my life.

To Mazen: My best friend, my life partner, my love. We've been together for over ten years now. An entire decade of joy, laughter, and growth. I can't wait to see what the upcoming years and decades will have in store for us. You are the sun in the solar system of my life. Thank you for loving me and supporting me in everything that I do.

To my firstborn: By the time this book comes out, you will be about two months old. You are going to irrevocably change my life, and even though no one is ever "ready" for parenthood, I am so ready to finally meet you. To hold you and watch you grow. To nurture you and guide you, to the best of my ability. I don't know what the future holds, but I promise you this: I will love you unconditionally. Always.

To everyone I've named and referenced, and to those I've somehow forgotten or omitted, but who have shaped my life in some way: Tigwicid. Thank you.

A NOTE FROM CYNTHIA LEITICH SMITH, AUTHOR AND CO-CURATOR OF HEARTDRUM

Dear Reader,

Sometimes life hits us with sudden loss, with unexpected limits that force us to shift our days and dreams. Before we know it, we're on a new journey. Though Maisie struggles with the aftermath of her ballet injury, she is quietly building strength through the support of her family, and through her connection to her ancestors and to our natural world.

As with many Native stories, author Christine Day illuminates Maisie's full humanity, with all the emotions that come with it, through the lens of daily life. The sweet promise of waffles, the ocean mist rising from a whale, the magical shimmer of snowflakes, the forever love of a father lost and of a father found, the bittersweet void of an unanswered text to a friend. . . .

In the ebb and flow of time, in moments that are quiet and laughing and aching and awe-inspiring, we're all like Maisie in that we experience pain, healing, and hope for the future.

Have you read many stories by and about Native people? No doubt *The Sea in Winter* will inspire you to read more. The novel is published by Heartdrum, a Native-focused imprint of HarperCollins Children's Books, which offers stories about young Native heroes by Native and First Nations authors and illustrators. I'm honored to include this book on our first list because of the honesty in its tenderness, and because Maisie's story shows that we all are stronger, deeper, and more courageous heroes than we can sometimes imagine.

There's more than one way to dance. No matter the challenge, each of you, like Maisie, contains boundless potential and an infinity of possibilities for brighter days to come.

Mvto,
Cynthia Leitich Smith

IN 2014, We Need Diverse Books (WNDB) began as a simple hashtag on Twitter. The social media campaign soon grew into a 501(c)(3) nonprofit with a team that spans the globe. WNDB is supported by a network of writers, illustrators, agents, editors, teachers, librarians, and book lovers, all united under the same goal—to create a world where every child can see themselves in the pages of a book. You can learn more about WNDB programs at www.diversebooks.org.

CHRISTINE DAY (Upper Skagit) grew up in Seattle, nestled between the sea, the mountains, and the pages of her favorite books. Her debut novel, *I Can Make This Promise*, was a best book of the year from *Kirkus Reviews*, *School Library Journal*, NPR, and the Chicago Public Library, as well as a Charlotte Huck Award Honor Book and an American Indian Youth Literature Award Honor Book. *The Sea in Winter* is her second novel. Christine lives in the Pacific Northwest with her family.

CYNTHIA LEITICH SMITH is the bestselling, acclaimed author of books for all ages, including *Rain Is Not My Indian Name*, *Indian Shoes*, *Jingle Dancer*, and *Hearts Unbroken*. She is the author-curator of Heartdrum, a Native-focused imprint at HarperCollins Children's Books, and is on the core faculty of the MFA program in writing for children and young adults at Vermont College of Fine Arts. She is an enrolled member of the Muscogee (Creek) Nation and lives in Austin, Texas.

MICHAELA GOADE is an award-winning illustrator and member of the Tlingit tribe. She is the illustrator of recent picture books *We Are Water Protectors* by Carole Lindstrom, *Encounter* by Brittany Luby, and *Shanyaak'utlaax: Salmon Boy*, winner of the 2018 American Indian Youth Literature Best Picture Book Award. She grew up in the rainforest and on the beaches of Southeast Alaska and continues to make her home on traditional Tlingit land today.

Turn the page for a peek at
Christine Day's debut novel,

I CAN MAKE THIS PROMISE!

1.

THE BIG BANG

July 4

Fireworks are banned in my neighborhood. There are too many trees, too many houses. So this year for the Fourth of July, my parents are taking me to the Tulalip reservation, about twenty miles north of the city. They sell all kinds of fireworks, and they have a huge field where you can set them off. This place is crowded and colorful and chaotic. It's amazing.

My parents lead the way to the booths. There's a food truck parked beside the big gravel lot, selling authentic Mexican tacos. The smell of cooked, seasoned meat fills the air, mixing with the peppery gunpowder from all the fireworks. I can practically *feel* it, in little flecks of grime all over my skin.

Mom asks, "Do you need these, Edie?" She opens her palm, revealing a little package of earplugs.

I shake my head. "I'm okay, thanks."

The booths are set up in several rows. The nearest one is decorated with red, white, and blue streamers, and a huge banner that shouts "FIRE-WORKS" in bold letters. The booth across from it is lime green, with little alien heads and UFOs outlined all over it in black paint. Another is hot pink, with candy-colored rockets arranged in bouquets on its counter. The next is blue, with the Seattle Seahawks logo stenciled in stark white and silver, plus the number 12; the 1 is shaped like the Space Needle.

I like this graffiti. I like the bright colors, the bold lines. I wonder if they created drawings and stencils first, or if they just grabbed their cans of spray paint and improvised. I also wonder if they keep sketchbooks, or have favorite places to draw, like I do. I'm always curious about other artists and their habits, their unfinished drafts, their inspirations.

As we keep moving, I can't help but drink it all in. I've never been to a reservation before. Each person I make eye contact with feels significant. It's possible some of them are distant relatives. I could be walking past cousins or aunties right now, and I wouldn't even know it.

A rock-and-roll version of "The Star-Spangled Banner" starts blaring out of nowhere, and I glance around myself, trying to find the speakers. But as the loud electric guitar mimics the sounds of "O say, can you see?" I instead notice a food vendor with signs that say they have traditional Native American fry bread.

I stop and stare. The line is huge. The menu is handwritten on a whiteboard. An ice-filled cooler contains sodas and bottled lemonades. There are two open counters—one where you pay, one where you wait for your order. I watch as a girl receives her food. The fry bread is a rumpled, golden-brown disk, served on a paper plate. It almost looks like an elephant ear.

As the guitar transitions to a choppy "What so proudly we hailed—" something knocks into the backs of my legs. I stumble and turn around. A dog peers up at me with watery, bloodshot eyes. He's panting hard, and his fur is mangy, but he looks happy. Surprisingly calm. I thought all dogs hated fireworks, but he doesn't seem to mind the noise, the chaos. He just looks a little lost.

I extend my hand to him. "Hi, puppy."

He lifts his big nose. Sniffs my fingers. Pushes his snout against my palm. His tail wags ferociously as he inches closer.

"That's a good boy," I say. "You're a good boy."

I check his neck, but he isn't wearing a collar.

I glance around. Cash registers chime, and shouts of laughter are eclipsed by a huge *boom*. Shoes crunch across the gravel. A group of men walk by in mismatched basketball jerseys. A teenager adjusts her sunglasses; her colorful, beaded bracelets slide down her brown forearm. A guy with two long, dark braids is wearing a Batman tank top. A toddler is mid-meltdown, hands clamped over her ears, face crumpled as she cries out.

"Poor thing," I murmur. I stroke the dog's head, distracted. "Where's your owner?"

The rock-and-roll version of "The Star-Spangled Banner" is no longer recognizable. The guitar riffs have dissolved into wails. It doesn't sound like "O'er the ramparts we watched." It doesn't sound like anything. Just crashing notes and frantic energy.

I turn in the other direction, and an older woman catches my gaze and holds it. She's seated on a stool at the edge of the crowd. Her T-shirt bears the message "Find Our Missing Girls." Huh. I wonder what that's about.

"Edie?" Mom's voice cuts in through the blaring guitar and blasting fireworks. "What are you doing?" She places her hand on my shoulder and gently steers me away. "Honey, you can't pet random dogs like that. It's not safe. Look at how big he is. He might hurt you."

Dad's behind her. "Your mother's right. I know he's cute, but you need to be careful."

"But he's alone," I say. "Shouldn't we help him find his way home?"

"Someone will come along for him," Mom says, and I can barely hear her as the guitar screeches. "Don't worry."

She tugs me away, but I look back. The dog sits in the middle of the walkway. His ears perk up, and his tongue lolls out of the corner of his mouth as he watches me leave.

• • •

Great books by
CHRISTINE DAY!

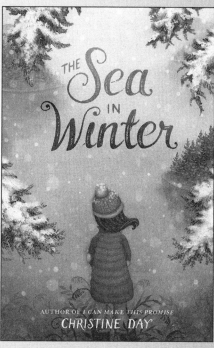